Le Journal

AN

Angela Fournier

ADVENTURE THRILLER SERIES

BOOK FOUR

A NOVELLA

John F Russo

John's Fictional Novels

The Perplexity of Engram
(A futuristic fable)

Enjoy Angela Fournier
Adventure Thriller Series
in
Tabula Rasa – Book One
Darkness After Midnight – Book Two
Compromised Interests – Book Three
Le Journal – *A Novella* – Book Four

Other titles in this series coming soon!
Whiteburn – Book Five
(Including excerpts from Le Journal)

Books2Read:
https://books2read.com?ap/8prE7z/John-F-Russo
Instagram: @johnfrussoauthor
Website: https://johnfrussoauthor.com
FB: JF Russo

Disclaimer

Sale of this book without a front cover may be unauthorized. If this book is coverless, it may have been reported to the publisher as "unsold or destroyed" and neither the author nor the publisher may have received payment for it.

Angela Fournier – Le Journal Book Four is a work of fiction. Names, characters, businesses, organizations, places, events and incidents are the products of the author's imagination or are used fictitiously. Any resemblance to actual events, locales, or persons, living or dead, is entirely coincidental.

Artwork: John Russo

E-book ISBN-13: 978-1-7346457-9-8

Paperback ISBN-13: 978-1-7346457-8-1

E-book release 2022 - Revised 2024
Print release 2024

Dedicated Always

To

My loving wife, Lori Russo

To

My Belgium-born grandmother, Claire Marie Joseph Sonnet, who during the First World War, met my English grandfather, fell in love, married, and after the war, moved to Canada. To you, *ma grand-mère*, I dedicate this novella.

Acknowledgements

Thank you to my wife, Lori for her continuous input.

To my editor: Malory Wood of The Missing Ink for all her hard work and patience.

FN – Fabrique Nationale ®; Luger Pistol ®

Front Cover:

Leather Bound Journal – Rustic Town Store

Lock: GTHER – Chinese Character Combination Vintage Lock and Butterfly Latch

Pen: Wordsmith & Black Fountain Pen @wordsworthandblack

Content

From the Author

The inspiration to write Le Journal coincided with my own desire to explore my Italian ancestry. Written with respect following the writings of the early 1940s and the history of World War II, we delve back to the beginning of the code name "The Swan" or, in French, *"La Cygne"*. The *Résistance* used names of animals to hide their true identity in case of capture and questioned by the Gestapo. In my previous manuscripts, this name has surfaced without clarification. In this novella, the *nom de guerre* — La Cygne — is revealed. Is there a possible link to Angela? If so, will she believe?

Introduction

She had wit, beauty, intelligence and a certain boldness exceeded only by her strong convictions for a woman who had just turned seventeen years young on January 23, 1941. Some might have said that she was more obstinate when she had questioned authorities about her eligibility to attend medical school in Paris during such tumultuous times. After all, the Nazis had walked right into Paris on June 14, 1940.

These qualities had not been lost on academic rhetoric but observed. In fact, she was guided with equal enthusiasm, pushed to her limits and then some. For Claire Marie Sonnet, this is what she lived for. Until — one day in June 1941, while sitting next to a pond on a concrete abutment feeding white, long-neck geese under the shadow of the Eiffel Tower, a gentleman approached her. His politeness earned him a seat next to her. A conversation ensued with particular mentioning of her support for a great cause and a chance at defending France. Apprehension flushed over her but was quickly dissolved by her suitor's observance, persuasiveness, and a promise of financial support for her continued medical studies — if she so desired.

She accepted.

Angela Fournier – Le Journal

Le Journal

Paris: 23 Janvier 1942 - 20:10 Heures

A cloud of lazy smoke hung in the air of the underground bunker as a chosen gathering of the elite commanders of the Third Reich beheld another propaganda film produced by the prevaricator, Joseph Goebbels. Sitting among the audience, a Panzer commander, *SS-Brigadeführer* Maximillian von Weißermann observed the spectacle in the dim light. He strained to listen, twitching his ears like a dog might as a discerning sound bit at them and their memory-recall placed it on an invisible ribbon, fast forwarding the message and stopping at that exact frequency of recall. Von Weißermann imagined all that in a split second as his mind found that frequency like an animal might and the images were displayed in 16mm black and white sequences. The words trumpeted like notes from the brass flutes of marching men; stiff-legged, erect, and arms straight as an arrow, in sync, swinging like pendulums. Only then did he sense the danger of those words.

Von Weißermann rose from his chair and walked through the projected light-beam, which casted his silhouette against the pitted wall — a barren wall with little color. He excused himself with a grunt, muffling his words with his hand, and twisted the knob with the other. A red glare striped the backs of those who remained as the door opened wider. A caged light, mounted high, passed its muted brilliance to the next and to the next in succession, until at the end of the hall, a metal door, heavier than the one before and marked by two armed men, one on each side, snapped their heels together in unison — crisp.

On the outside, von Weißermann stood and reached for his cigarettes and lit one with the flip of his gold-plated flame, a gift from the *Führer*, and returned the matching set to his breast pocket of his black outer-coat. He shuddered with the cold. His breath, frozen in mid-air, barely rose above the sandbagged entrance. He placed his cap on his head just so and fingered his black leather gloves. Two drags from his cigarette, and then a four-door sedan pulled next to him with headlights taped with only an inch of illumination piercing the darkness. He stepped on the fag with his black shiny boot snuffing the ash into a melting liquid. He climbed into the back seat.

A young dark-haired French woman, Marta Savant, wearing a floppy hat cocked to the side and veiled, dressed in a full-length fur and made-up with red lips — 'delicious red lips' as he had said — and powdered skin, sat to the side. As he, Maximillian von Weißermann, the man whom she despised, stepped in, she only hinted with a quirk of a smile.

The street lamps were barren of light and as von Weißermann sat next to her, his hand parted the fur and rested on her nyloned leg. Marta pulled a compact from her fur's pocket, opened it and moved it about to light her face and to admire her painted reflection. She pursed her lips, and with her index finger, touched each side of her lips at the corners, removing any flaw of lipstick bleed. Marta closed the compact and replaced it into the fur's pocket next to her Fabrique Nationale .25 caliber semi-automatic pistol. Her look was not at him but stared out of the rear quarter window at the white-capped porches. Neither spoke while the driver maneuvered through the rutted, snow-covered street as they headed northwest on *Boulevard Garibaldi* to the bridge — *Pont de Passy*.

The tiered bridge lay empty, abandoned only to them. A hundred yards ahead, a shaded, barn-style caged red light shone, and another, a hundred yards from the first. The driver straddled the tracks, stopped, and then stepped out and went to the front of the vehicle. He maneuvered a lever through a series of gears and notches and lowered a set of steel-flanged rims onto the track. The driver stepped back into the near-warmth of the interior and shifted the sedan into gear. They slowly crossed the *Seine*.

Von Weißermann's mid-night blue eyes, hinting to black, darted, anticipating, as he watched the driver maneuver the vehicle along the tracks. Von Weißermann mentioned a name, Singstad, the tunnel man, the man that built great tunnels, a man he respected for his engineering brilliance. After a failed attempt was made at blowing up a tunnel named *Waasland* by the retreating Belgium army, von Weißermann's perseverance was honored by another medal being added to his chest. He disliked having to travel through that tunnel, any tunnel, not just that tunnel, like a rat — a river rat, crossing not knowing what had entered from the other end or whether he would reach the other end. The driver downshifted, they slowed. The clanging of metal-on-metal, rims-to-rails, melted the ice and the noise echoing against the inner wheel-wells warned everyone in Paris they approached. Their car turned right onto *Avenue de Tokio* and von Weißermann watched the Eiffel Tower as it stared down on him. They rounded *Jardins du Trocadéro* and headed to *Avenue Kléber*.

This was not his land nor his home nor his people. He had said, *"This was a madman's dream and one that could not be supported from his Fatherland for any amount of perceptual time, no matter whose design."*

The driver pulled over and stopped at the smooth, granite-cut block building, which had an attached overhanging marquee, where men hovered on this cold street to catch a glimpse. For Marta Savant, it was not like the *Stadsfeetzaal* in *Antwerp* with its glass, gold-leafed dome and oak parquet floors where flash bulbs would burn away in a flurry and young women and young men would clamber over each other and push and shove and hand her a pen with that night's handbill to sign.

Von Weißermann waited for the driver to open the door and when he did, Maximillian stepped out first and he, the truculent SS Brigadeführer Maximillian von Weißermann was saluted — heels snapped and arms raised. "*SIEG HEIL*", they said. The Brigadeführer turned to Marta and offered his hand as her nyloned leg swung to view and then her other leg swung out and the young men shouted in a language she didn't want to understand but whose intentions she well imagined. The wind toiled with her hat and she placed her hand upon it to prevent it from being pitched into the air. And he placed his arm about her as Marta bent forward to brave the wind and they stepped through the open door of the occupied Majestic Hôtel. Above, on the marquee, displayed: ***Heute Nacht Fräulein* Marta Savant**.

The lobby smelt of stale smoke and sauerkraut and the combined smells offended her, making Marta nauseous. The curtain she had eyed were made of SS flags draping the distance from ceiling to floor, and the dining room's tables and chairs were re-arranged for this engagement to form a circular stage in the center for the SS benefit. Perverted eyes lashed at her coat, stripping Fräulein Savant naked before she even stepped to the floor. Von Weißermann directed Marta to a small dressing room made from a previously-used storage locker and upon arriving, he opened her dressing room door — she stepped inside.

"*Fünf Minuten*," he said, and then he closed the door behind her giving her privacy.

Marta stood there and looked around — soiled walls stained from wooden shelves that once supported a chattel of wares, a coat rack with a red sequin dress with tassels hung on a hanger and a small table supported a mirror propped up against the wall. A single clear bulb hung from the ceiling and stopped just above the mirror and the reflected light highlighted long silk evening gloves dangling over the table's edge. Marta reached for the chair that sat lonely to the side and it supported her as she hung her head for a brief moment of clarity. Raising her head, she let the fur slide off her shoulders to the floor, and, dressed in only her modest lingerie, she removed her black brassiere and reached for the dress. At a proper venue, she would have matched her undergarment to the dress but for these SS cullions, Marta would let them think, for a brief moment, that what they saw was her naturalness.

21:00 Heures

That very night, a short distance away where the four gilt-bronze statues of *Fames* stood dark and frozen with a sheet of ice hiding their anonymity, seven men crossed in the shadows of the ornate *Pont Alexandre* III's deck. It had been perceived as a dumb idea — as dumb as hell of an idea — but many battles throughout history had been won by the element of surprise. No one would attempt such a maneuver as this, not even the *Résistance Maquis*.

The seven men crept along the rail hidden under white-woven blankets, each moving quickly and autonomously. The frozen snow squeaked under their laced up high-top boots. Each rubber sole imprinted the outer crust, their existence then swept away by the blowing snow. Their distance to their objective was far and on foot extremely dangerous. Each knew the plan and the dangers of that plan.

The bank of the river's edge, visible between the bolsters, was part of the plan until they had to break for the streets. The wind swept the lighter dryer snow with a vengeance, giving the men further disguise — but the iced slopes caused grave concern if one might slip. To add to the liquidity of their plan, these seven brave men had to be weary of the R-boats that patrolled the Seine. Past patriots had been picked from the river and shot on-sight against the cold concrete banks. Their bodies had been left to rot to discourage others of the *Résistance*.

7

. . .

Marta tilted the mirror and stood back, and then backed away yet farther and turned just so, from her left to her right and bent to align her nylons. She gathered the material of one and then the other to ensure matching the black seam to the center of her curvy calves. She straightened to adjust the garter in front where it peeked out from the slit in the dress. A knock and then a voice said, "Fräulein?"

"*Une moment s'il vous plaît*," Marta said rather pleasantly, understanding full well of the recourse.

21:15 Heures

The men reached the other side of Pont Alexandre to the district of *Champs-Élysées* — and tucked underneath the *socle* that supported the grand columns to the underbelly of the bridge. They huddled together in silence and synchronized their watches, each double-checking the magazines of their automatic Sten guns. One man, Gage Fabre, the man with steel-grey eyes, looked at the bag he was carrying and said, "*Mes amies*, if I do not make it, one of you must carry on. Leave me if you must but carry on. Do you understand?" "*Oui,*" the six whispered in compliance.

. . .

Marta pulled on the long gloves just past her elbows and with one last quick look in the mirror, she turned toward the door. The crystal knob shattered her image into a tapestry of color against the bleak walls as she turned it. The paneled door opened to the hallway to the waiting Maximillian. He looked into her eyes like he was prepared to say something but hesitated. He instead patted Marta on her *derrière*.

"Maxi, please walk me to the center of that wolf pack."

"I have to leave you here, my darling. Break a leg," he said wistfully.

Marta looked at him concerned, and then he sported a smile, his smile, but his eyes did not lie, she sensed he had... he had just said goodbye.

"After the show then, Maxi. You come and rescue me."

"If your admirers haven't surrounded you, I will do my best. But before you go, I have something for you."

Max reached into his starched coat and pulled out a modest-in-size, decorative wooden box and opened it. Lying inside on the white satin interior was an Egyptian-blue velvet choker with an Ivory-carved Lady Luck cameo inlaid on an oval peach-colored stone. It was incased with a rim of gold and surrounded with delicate arches of etched platinum. He removed it and Marta turned with her back to him as Maximillian drew it over her head and attached it to the

9

slenderness of her neck. She touched the face of this brooch and he spread his hands along her bare shoulders.

"It is for good luck, my love. It is inscribed on back, but later after the show, you can read it."

Without saying a word, Marta turned and fixed her strut into motion as she had learned to do. Stepping from behind the curtain of flags, her hips sang with each step in a rhythmic triad and as Marta's legs crossed one in front of the other, her foot stopped for an instant like a staccato. She then sashayed toward the men in black and their guests, and bending to them, Marta caressed their drooling chins.

Muffled trumpets swooned and clarinets lightly dazzled on the high notes as their mistress of the night approached the microphone.

Von Weißermann looked behind to the kitchen's paneled door now being opened by a waiter with slick, closely-cropped hair and sporting a moustache, waxed and twisted at the ends. He gestured with a wink and von Weißermann followed. The waiter placed his finger to his lips as other servers milled about filling demands from the SS officers engaged in the performance. They went through another door to where a private back room led to a set of stairs to the basement and a barred exterior door. It was left unlocked.

"Are they downstairs?"

"Not yet, Brigadeführer," said the moustached waiter.

Von Weißermann nervously looked at his watch. "I don't like it. There are too many SS officers mingling amongst them. They will know... the *Führer* will know."

"Are you worried about him or the girl? She knows very well her mission."

"Maybe, but she doesn't know it was I who betrayed her and that it is I who is sending her to her death. She doesn't know it was me who contacted you English. I didn't want her distracted. Even in the SS we have spies that watch us."

"We have to do this, you know it. If they get the V-1 off the ground by summer, England is in a whole lot of trouble. If your information is correct, it has to be now. Everyone in close contact with that mad scientist, von Braun, is here tonight."

"Yes...yes...yes, I know that. Don't humiliate me further. Let me know when they get here. I will go to the curtain and no farther."

21:30 Heures

In the Paris night, like rabbits the seven men moved, hopping from one spot to another, hidden behind wraps of rope and buttresses that secured smaller vessels. The night was cold and no one and their dog were out strolling about. The hatches were tight and their stacks smelt of dirty oil, thick and black. The men made their way along the docks to a set of steps that led to *Avenue Tokio*. They gathered again, huddled, aware, and they shed their white blankets and tucked their weapons under their over-coats. Two, then one, Fabre went next, then one more and the last two waited for their turn. It was quiet except for the wind whistling like the strings of a Stradivarius between the buildings, sweet of sound if this was not a night of deadly consequence. The men stepped like dockhands might returning from the sea in search of their favorite cabaret – quickly and determined.

A soldier stood in the protection of a shop's alcove in front of a barred door and removed his gloves to strike a match and placed his hands about it to shield it from the wind. Bent to the wind, two men quickly passed without noticing the sulking soldier. A furl of smoke rose between the slanted white crystals as he stepped out from his hiding with his rifle raised and poised on those who passed.

"*HALT!*" he shouted to be heard over the wind. The two men stopped and raised their hands in show of compliance and sense of cooperation. The soldier stepped closer. "You have papers?"

"*Oui*, in my coat," one offered.

"Turn around," said the soldier. The men eyed each other and slowly turned with cigarettes hanging from their mouths.

"This is my last fag. Do you have a couple to get me through this wretched night?"

"*Oui, der soldat*. I have extra." The man who spoke reached into his pocket of his outer-coat. "Here, take the pack. I'll get more if I need them at the cabaret."

"*Danke!*" said the soldier reaching out for the fags. Silently and from behind the soldier, one of the *Réseau* fighters pulled his knife and with quick concise strokes plunged his dagger deep between the shoulder blades of the soldier. Quickly they gathered him and placed him on the ground in the recess of the shop next to the barred entrance. Fabre caught up to them.

"I had no choice," said the knife-wielding man.

"You did well, Daniel. For a young man, you were very perceptive. Let's keep going. Only a few more blocks," said Fabre.

. . .

The boisterous clatter of yelling men could barely be heard over the thundering heeled boots desecrating the Majestic's wooden-planked floor. "*Mes Généraux et mes Scientifiques estime,*" Marta announced over her microphone. They quietened to her command. "You know my friend,

Mademoiselle Baker of great fame..." The patrons once again cheered and whistled like young schoolboys. She knew she had their attention. "I will do one of her most famous songs from 1930, *J'ai Deux Amours*."

21:45 Heures

The *Réseau* fighters took to the alley behind the Majestic and jostled between windswept garbage cans and frozen cardboard boxes to the door with the lettering: **Majestic**. From under their outer-coats, they pulled their Sten guns that the Résistance had received from an air-drop by the British SOE. Daniel was the first to enter. He pressed his ear to the inner door and motioned for the rest to enter and to head down the stairs. One by one they swiftly and quietly took the stairs with Fabre and his pack guarded from each direction. Daniel brushed the collective snow gathered from their boots down the open stairwell to the concrete floor below. Wooden barrels full of olives, cases of rum, racks of cloth-covered cheeses and bins of fruit lined the walls. Down the dimly-lit hallway they went and at the end, a steel padlocked door with a barred window awaited them. Fabre rushed to the door as his men took up posts hidden by the decadents of the Third Reich.

Bristol, the code name for the British SOE agent dressed in a waiter's outfit with slicked back hair and moustache, waxed and twisted at the ends, opened the inner door to the private room where he noticed the outer door had been closed tight. He treaded down the stairs and at its end, he rounded the railing and headed down the hall. He only saw one man in the dim light at the end — at the steel door.

"Frenchie," he whispered, "where are your men?" Alternately, they stood. Their Sten guns raised poised at him. He gulped. "Okay, gents," he said. "The weather is beautiful in the south at this time of year. I'm Bristol." They lowered their weapons.

"Do you have the key?" Fabre briskly asked.

"Yes...yes. Hang on mate. I thought you would've been here a half hour ago. The Krauts will want to see some skin soon. I don't know how many more songs she can sing before they become annoyed."

"The travel was not easy. Come, hurry with the key."

"Here it is." Bristol handed the key to Fabre who inserted it into the lock. It sprung open with a defying *click*. Fabre, Bristol and two other men went inside while the others stayed hidden at their posts. Fabre removed the contents from his duffle bag for the first time and laid it on the floor.

"What is this?" asked Fabre.

"Aye, we got it from the Yanks. New stuff. It's a Baratol type, a mixture of TNT and Barium nitrate and something called RDX. It is more stable, quicker-acting and more powerful. Secure them on the support beams with this tape and then we will tie them together with the igniter. I have to get back upstairs before I am missed. Can you handle this?"

"Yes, of course," said Fabre.

"Get your men to the exit door and out before you turn this switch. All hell will break loose."

"What about you?"

"I've got a safe room. Don't worry; I'm no hero, just doing my job. Take care, Frenchie. You have five minutes."

Bristol, continuing his ruse as a waiter, arrived upstairs with several bottles of Cognac in his hands to the chant of "TAKE IT OFF ... TAKE IT OFF". He had to hurry to von Weißermann — he had to know.

Von Weißermann only needed one look — that look on the waiter coming through the door with his hurried expression on his face. Bristol stepped to the storage room. Von Weißermann knew and he quickly stepped from behind the curtain and looked at Marta Savant.

As she spun around, her dress billowed. They jeered excessively. And then — her eyes caught his. Marta froze. Silence in her mind. She knew. Her dress whipped across her knees.

~

At 21:59 hours, Fabre turned the switch. The seven men were thrown through the exit door to the snow-covered alley. They hesitated a fraction too long.

The erupting interior hurled the patrons up, off the wooden-planked floor, which then blew into deadly flying projectiles. Glass shattered into crystal spears and embedded into the SS curtain, shredding it. The tables flew through the air and bodies were impaled by its parts. Screams were non-existent over the noise of the blast. Bodies lay about, disfigured and bloodied. Some staggered out the main door without consciousness, in wonder, perplexed with what had just happened.

Von Weißermann had been thrown against the kitchen's door by the blast wave and sunk to the splintered floor. Stunned, he managed to prop himself up and he swayed through the carnage to the hole in the floor. His uniform was frayed and blood dripped off his chin from an eight-inch splinter that had pierced his jaw. He hunted for her like a wild animal. He had not always loved her — he had taken her against her will — and now he loved her. He loved her more than life itself. He slid down a smoldering plank. He tossed aside bodies, their faces whitewashed in misery and their eyes bulging, until he saw a red tassel buried beneath — and then, a red glove. And again, he tossed one of these bodies aside to find her breathing — barely — but alive. He bent down to her to lift her up when a voice shouted, "*Verräter!*"

A one-armed officer, having just lost his other, held up his Lugar and was pointing it at the suspected traitor. Von Weißermann reached for his pistol but he was not fast enough. The officer shot once and then twice. Maximillian fell to his knees, his hand holding hers. A burst of shots rang out from behind von Weißermann and the one-armed officer slumped to his side.

Fabre had rushed back into the Majestic to the edge of the chaos to finish his objective when he saw a one-armed man shoot a SS officer who was holding onto a woman's hand. He set off a burst of fire-power killing the one-armed man. He swung his Sten gun to his side and slid down a smoldering plank. Fabre side-stepped the fallen bodies and knelt beside the SS commander. With his last breath, the SS commander whispered into Fabre's ear. "Please man, take her, and keep her safe. She has valuable informa..." His head slouched forward. Fabre gathered the woman into his arms and with Daniel's help, Fabre climbed out of the pit of death. Daniel directed Fabre and the lifeless woman to the storage room — and behind the table with a propped up mirror, a discovered shaft led to safety.

22:15 Heures

Fabre, unbeknownst to him, had taken the unconscious Fräulein Marta Savant down a planked slide to the building adjacent, through the dinge of the coal room — air thick and dusty. They passed the tentacles of massive round tubes wrapped at the joints by dissolving tape and escaping hot air, toward an excavated hole in the double-lined brick, to the building next to it. He rushed the stairs that led upward to another closed door. She remained in his arms oblivious to his struggle. Daniel had led the way and his patience was thin and his experience meager as he turned the crystal knob eagerly. A man wearing an Aegean wool cap pulled down over his slick hair and sporting a moustache, waxed and twisted at the ends, offered his hand. Startled, they recognized his face.

"This way, Frenchie. What the hell you doing here? You should have been blocks away by now."

Fabre moved to the hallway and propped himself up against the wall with his burden weighing heavy in his arms.

"Oh Frenchie, I don't know about her. I think she may be bad luck for you," said Bristol.

"We can't leave her. It would be certain death for her."

"Where are you going to take her?"

"To *Vichy*. She'll be safe there."

"Okay, your funeral. I have a truck coming. It should be here in two hours filled with supplies for the Gestapo. On their return, you can take her in that, if you wish."

"Thank you, I owe you a great debt, Bristol."

19

"Thank me after the war. For now, I'll do what I can. Keep her quiet until we get out of here. Are there more with you?"

"No, just Daniel and I. I sent the others away. Maybe all of their footprints in the snow will sour the Gestapo's taste to look further within these buildings."

"Correction... who in their right mind would stay in these buildings so close to the explosion? I'll let you know when it is safe to come out. We only use this building for storage and the *Krauts* know that. I'll fetch you in a couple of hours if all goes well."

"Thank you, Bristol."

Daniel removed his hat and nodded out of respect as the SOE agent took leave. And Fabre, a strong man as he was, also nodded with respect. They squatted next to the wood-burning stove in the unused kitchen where the iron grate on the floor allowed the warmer air of the furnace below to filter up. Daniel covered the woman with her fur that he had been carrying and a *clunk* sounded as the fur met the floor. He checked the pockets and found a compact and a loaded FN .25 caliber semi-automatic pistol. He replaced it from where he found it as it was not his. He was no thief. It was hers for her protection and he was a man and he could handle himself with his knife.

"Daniel, look around quietly and see if you can find some clothes for her, anything will do. This mangled red dress will be of no use or disguise for her. Man's trousers it does not matter... anything that we can dress her in. A shirt as well to cover her breasts that no man should witness them and further shame her, she does not need that."

"*Oui, mon oncle*, I will do as you ask and know as you know. I feel the same and will hide her from eyes that don't know her as we know what she has suffered."

"Go now, Daniel. She begins to shiver and I am fearful she may awake in a stranger's arms and not take too kindly as she lays bare to us."

Fabre gently laid the woman's head from his lap down to the floor and moved quietly as to not disturb her. He removed his scarf and tried the hot water tap at the sink and there was none. He turned the squeaky cold water tap and a mere dribble escaped, enough to wet his scarf and no more. He returned to her side and carefully wiped her face of blood and debris. He took each arm and did the same and he placed her tattered dress about her to hide her from embarrassment. He removed her necklace and placed it in the inner pocket of her fur coat. Her airways need not be hampered by such a thing.

Daniel returned with excitement bearing a workman's shirt, although dusted with coal, and a pair of bibbed pants — also dusted with coal — and a large pair of rubber boots.

"Good find, Daniel. You did well. Your eyes are meant for the one you love but we are in need to work as one, so help

21

me remove her tattered dress and restore these garments of a workman to cover her. Lift her gently so I may slip off her dress. Good. Now lift each leg separately so I may insert them into the hollow of the pant and roll the hind end under her *derrière*. Good, Daniel. Now hand me the shirt and lift her torso so I can slide it under her and insert one arm at a time. Let not more be said to others, but she has a fine form of any woman I have seen."

Fabre fastened the buttons and secured the straps of the bib over her shoulders and buttoned them to the face of the bib. He gathered the extra material of the bulky fabric and folded it around her ankles and slipped the over-sized boots onto her bare feet. He raised her head and gently placed it into his lap once more. As Marta lay prone on the floor and Fabre sat with his back against the stove he had one more request. "Okay, Daniel, place her fur about her to keep her warm. We shall wait together for the truck."

23:15 Heures

Fabre and Daniel had closed their eyes and laid in a light sleep. Fabre had his Sten gun resting on his chest and next to him remained the lifeless Marta Savant. Daniel lay with a Lugar he had removed from a dead, one-armed officer. The wind howled and seeped through the bricks carrying white crystals that mounted in a cluster on the wood-planked floor at the exposed crack. The German air raids of June 3, 1940, before their occupation of France, had significant consequence on the old mortar rattling its structure from dropped bombs.

A man approached from the front door, different than Bristol, and he was French of rugged build with a large scar from his eyebrow down to his chin, white against his bristled beard. He came to the kitchen and peered around the corner and quickly withdrew. He then spoke in a whisper.

"Fabre... Fabre, awake man! I'm Alfonso... to take you to Vichy."

Fabre startled, jumped up with his Sten gun pointing at the invisible voice.

"Who goes there?" said Fabre.

"I'm Alfonso. Bristol said to take you to Vichy. We need to go."

Daniel awoke and rolled with his Lugar also pointing at the voice coming from around the corner.

"Show yourself man, so we may believe you," said Fabre.

"Bristol sent me. Don't shoot! I'll show my face."

Alfonso rounded the corner with hands above his head and his pockets spilling with bread and cheese.

"I brought you food. Please, may I lower my arms?"

"Sorry, Alfonso. I am Gage Fabre and this is my nephew, Daniel. Yes, please come in."

They lowered their guns as Alfonso came into the dim light and had bread and cheese to offer. He looked down and saw the woman lying on the floor.

"Who is the woman?" he asked apprehensively.

"A patriot who was badly injured trying to help us."

"She cannot come with us in her state. No, no, no...," said Alfonso shaking his head as he looked at the lifeless woman. "Bristol did not say anything about this woman."

"She will certainly be harassed by the Gestapo if we do not protect her," said Fabre.

"How will we fit her into the empty barrels? She has no life to aid us."

"Daniel and I will take the risk to fold her into one. We cannot and will not leave her."

"Very well," said Alfonso, "...but if the *Krauts* start to harass me at the check points, I will plead ignorance as they know me as a simple truck driver who gives them cigarettes. These routes are imperative to supply the Résistance with arms and communication. You need to know that, man."

"I comprehend. She has valuable information that needs to be heard from her mouth," said Fabre. He looked Alfonso

24

straight in the eyes and said what he had said because he had made a promise.

"You have made your point, Fabre. I wish to argue no more, but she is your responsibility. Do we understand each other?"

"*Mais bien*, you are a good man of good heart," said Fabre. "Where shall we meet you?"

"It is complicated now. Boy, do you have papers?"

"*Oui*."

"That is good. The boy can ride up front with me as my helper. You cannot go out the front door as we, carrying this woman in your arms. I will stop on the street at the alley's entrance and you must take her through the alley without discovery. If a soldier comes, I will distract him as long as I can. Be careful, they are still sifting through the debris. Some men badly injured and some dead. I overheard the Commandant speaking of a riddle of bullets gouging the wall behind one of his lieutenants whose holster was empty and without pistol at his side — and the infamous SS von Weißermann dead with two bullets to his chest. Also, they found the partial remains of a red dress with no body. They are assuming she is one of the crispies and unidentifiable but the SS have very curious minds. I say this to you for your awareness," said Alfonso as he rolled his eyes towards the woman on the floor.

"I understand what you are implying. I will meet you as you say." Fabre turned to face his nephew and said, "Go, Daniel, and be safe."

"Mais, oncle?"

"No, Daniel, say no more. It is the only way to keep you safe. Now go with this man and trust his word."

Alfonso turned towards the hallway and with hesitation Daniel followed the man with the scarred face to the front of the building. The man opened the door and they stepped outside into the blizzard.

Fabre removed the fur from Marta's body and wrapped the strap of his Sten gun around the woman's head and draped it across her shoulder to hang at her back. He fitted her arms through the sleeves of the fur and pushed the buttons through its loops and then lifted her into his arms. Standing tall, Fabre adjusted her weight.

The rusty hinges of the back door *squealed* as he pushed it open, and out into the blizzard he went with the woman dangling in his arms. Three doors down, two soldiers stepped out of the rear entrance of the Majestic — the one that Fabre had entered with his men. The two soldiers huddled to light their cigarettes. Taking a deep drag, they looked up and saw Fabre weaving through the debris of wind-blown cans and frozen cardboard boxes.

"*Halt!*" yelled one of them. "What are you doing?" They both raised their weapons and stepped into the alley with the snow and the debris. Fabre put the woman down and leaned her against the wall and held her in place with one hand as he turned to the Germans singing as loud as he could.

"Ohhhh...! *M-o-n a-m-o-u-r...*"

"Shut your mouth, drunkard. Raise your arms!"

Fabre complied and the woman slid down the wall to as far as the frozen boxes allowed. They laughed.

"Hahaha, drunkard, take your whore and go back to your gutter; otherwise we might shoot your drunken ass as a spy for the Résistance."

Fabre bowed in grand gesture and toppled to one knee. The soldiers turned laughing at the misfit's misfortune. Fabre picked up the slouching woman stopped in time by the frozen boxes and he raised her into his arms and turned to face the end of the alley with no truck in sight.

He carried her through the drifts of knee-high snow to the beginning of the alley and to the open street where he saw a barricade manned by SS and Gestapo soldiers diverting the occasional traffic including, the truck with the man and the boy.

Fabre was on his own with a lifeless burden occupying his arms and his otherwise nimble strategies. He moved her to his shoulder and slung her over like a sack of potatoes, her hands braving the blizzard without gloves, dangling there cold and fragile.

Fabre followed the route in which they came and passed the alcove with the frozen soldier. He stopped. Placing his burden down on the iced concrete, he reached to the man's less-needed gloves and removed them from his frozen dead fingers. Fabre quickly covered his burden's fragile hands and rubbed them vigorously together and stretched over the soldier and removed his Lugar from his holster and placed it into his outer-coat's pocket. He looked from the alcove in each direction and shouldered the woman again and he headed for the docks.

. . .

Alfonso and Daniel cleared the Gestapo check-point but not without harassment. It didn't matter that they, the *Heer* soldiers, vouched for the innocence of the truck driver to the Gestapo. They were in charge and they ordered the *Heer* soldiers to break open the barrel lids. Disappointed with lack of discovery, the Gestapo let the truck pass.

"We need to go back for my uncle," the boy said as the truck driver shifted with a grind into 2nd gear.

"We have no chance tonight. If we return so suddenly they will know something is up. No, maybe tomorrow, but not tonight. It is too late to return tonight."

"Tomorrow then!" insisted Daniel.

"Maybe tomorrow, maybe not tomorrow... but maybe the next day if we do not return tomorrow." He shifted into 3rd gear.

"What will my uncle do? And he has that woman to slow him down!" shouted Daniel over the whine of the truck's engine.

"He knew, I know he knew, he understood the implications as he is a man of understanding and he knew the implications. I could see it in his eyes as we talked of the implications. He knew. I shall not talk anymore of these implications and you shall not mention it anymore tonight."

They bounced down the snow-rutted road.

24 Janvier 1942 - 01:20 Heures

Fabre, the man of understanding and great courage, felt fatigued by the time he and his burden reached the docks. Soon the light of the day would announce their implications to all and a few would report their maneuvers to the evil that surrounded Paris. *I must find safe passage*, he thought. *I have an obligation to save this woman and protect her from a certain performance with death that she had not asked for but had been thrust upon her because of another's will. That man's will and his light and his wisdom and his strength gone in a flash as he tried to save this woman from what he was not proud but what he understood had to be done. Was the German any different from me and his will and his understanding?*

He had been handed the life of another, thrust upon him by another man's will to save her and now he, Fabre, a Frenchman, had to serve the will of a German. She was young and beautiful and firm as he saw, but if it was another not so young and not so beautiful and not so firm, would he then share the same will of the German to protect her and do as the dying German begged? *Yes*, he thought, *I would do the same.*

The boards of the dock creaked with each step frozen still by its glazed coating, rasping with the weight of Fabre as he stepped as if howling to escape from their burden thrust upon them, their will, taken by the chilled wind from bending with ease and swaying to its natural rhythm. He found a barge with billowing oily-black soot escaping its smoke-stack and depositing that ilk-like ink drops on a fine white-wool sweater.

Fabre laid her upon her fur propped up against a cast iron piling dressed in turns of hemp rope that were bristled and chafed. He abandoned her, frail and unaware of his abandonment, and he stepped like a cat upon the deck of this barge. He pulled his Lugar and wrapped his scarf around the muzzle and knocked gingerly.

"Go away! We are in for the night, man."

He knocked again, this time a little harder after hearing the man's voice.

"What, man? Are you deaf? Be gone!"

Fabre pounded on the barge's hatch.

31

"By God man, who are you that bother us so?" The gruff man slid the hatch open to the barrel of a German Lugar stuck in his face.

"Step back, man. I care not to spill your blood on this fucking night but tempt me not."

The man slowly backed away as Fabre, persuasive in his manner, needed not to further insult this man and Fabre entered the light. They saw a strong man before them with steel-grey eyes with fire burning in them.

"What do you want of us?" asked a thin man with hands that looked bigger than the rest of his body.

"A safe haven and secured passage out of here."

"We cannot leave at this hour?" said the larger man.

"Why?" asked Fabre.

The thin man answered, "We don't have the daily charts from the Germans to where the mines are set. Each day they move them about and when we are summoned to bring supplies to them, it is at that time that they give us their positions."

"When do you leave again?" Fabre asked.

"Maybe tomorrow depending on the ice on the river, or maybe the next."

"When do they inform you of their need?"

"At six bells," said the thin man being very compliant to Fabre's questions.

"I mean you no harm but I have found a need to summon your help and your truth to secure safe passage out of Paris to where the river dips at its lowest. Will you help a fellow Frenchman?"

The two men looked at each other and back to the Lugar that was still pointing straight at them.

"For France and for a fellow Frenchmen, we will take you to where you ask. Close the hatch and come join us in some wine we borrowed from the Nazis," said the larger man, the man in-charge.

"There is one other complication..." Fabre put his pistol into his outer-coat's pocket and went back outside into the blizzard. He returned through the hatch with a bundle heaved over his shoulder. Fabre laid her down on one of the small cots. "...she must come too." The men gasped when he removed the fur that was hiding her face.

"What have you done, stranger? Have you molested her?"

"No... she has been still since I found her. I've been put in charge of her safety and must secure her safe passage away from Paris."

33

"But... but... she's the cabaret singer. The famous one," said the thin man.

"I don't know of what you speak. I found her in this condition and was summoned to save her."

"You do not know who she is, man?" said the larger man.

"No, I tell you. I know not who she is, only that of what I have told you."

"*Mon Dieu*, man! The Germans will be looking for her! She has become their *Fräulein*. This is Marta Savant."

Fabre looked at the woman, the woman he had stripped and saw her wonders and dressed her in workmen's clothing so no other stranger would harass her with their eyes — the woman he had almost gotten shot for, the one he had carried through the blizzard — and now to find out the Germans idolized her. That she was their Fräulein. He looked at the two stunned men who had stepped back, as if — if they stood closer to her, their involvement would be considered treasonous by the Nazis.

"It does not matter. She has suffered greatly and I have looked into the eyes of a dead man who summoned me to protect her. And I, as a Frenchman, will do what I must until my last breath. Do we understand this complication now set before us?"

"*Oui, monsieur*," they said in unison.

34

Fabre did not mince his words and as a strong man he said what he had to say. He opened her fur and unhooked the strap from his Sten gun and pulled it from under her. He emptied his pockets of bread and cheese given to him by the man called Alfonso, the man with the scar from his eyebrow to his chin. A man does not procure an injustice like that from hiding behind trees in the forest or buried in the tunnels that ran like a spider web under Paris.

"Give me wine to take the chill from my bones. Here is bread and cheese to share," said Fabre.

Fabre removed her rubber boots and blew into his hands and then he rubbed her feet vigorously again and again.

"Do you have extra wool socks I can cover her feet with?"

The thin man grabbed a pair that had been hung over a line drying near the smudge pot and gave them to Fabre. They were warm to the touch and dry. He covered her feet and slipped the rubber boots back on. Fabre got up from the edge of the cot and took a bench at the long narrow table where the wine, bread and cheese were displayed. The other two men took the bench on the other side of the long narrow table and together they broke bread.

"In a couple more hours it will be daylight. Do the Germans molest you if they have no need for your service?"

"No," said the thin man.

"Sometimes one will knock and ask for cigarettes," said the larger man.

"At six bells?" asked Fabre.

"No, later... maybe nine but no later than nine and a half."

"Good. We can drink this bottle and rest longer if we must," said Fabre in a joking fashion.

"Ah, man, you do have humor behind those eyes."

Fabre's face did not change with the larger man's remark but instead, he stood and removed his outer-coat and went to the woman and placed it upon her for further warmth. The small cabin was warm to him and he removed his inner jacket and then his sweater and he still stood as he rolled his sleeves up his forearms. The larger man observed a long scar on Fabre's left forearm and as Fabre sat and took his wine with his left hand, the larger man observed the scar went to his fingers.

"What happened?" said the larger man nodding with his head towards the injustice.

"An accident," said Fabre, flatly.

"Yes, one would assume that to be the truth but is there a story of such?"

Fabre took another large gulp of wine from his glass and filled it again before passing the bottle to the others.

"I was fixing a German track-car that we had seized and had to weld the heavy gun back onto its mount. I was in a hurry because we got word the Germans had summoned more men and had found courage to come after us. I grabbed a grinder and replaced a grinding wheel of slower speed to what the grinder turned and when I touched the wheel to where I was in position to weld, the wheel of the grinder broke apart and cut through my fingers and traveled up my forearm and leaped into the air off of my shoulder just missing my face. The grinder fell to the floor and with its wire, it turned in circles like a mad dog might that has been infected by the disease and because he loves his master and knows that it's the disease that makes him ill. But his love for his master makes him turn in circles to protect his master from his bite."

"You had a dog like that?" asked the thin man.

"No... I am saying it was like that of which a mad dog would do who loved his master."

They each took another large swallow of wine and filled their glasses again. The wine warmed their insides. The larger man reached around behind him and from a bin, he pulled two more bottles and set them on the table. He popped the cork of one and re-filled the dwindling level of red liquid and returned the bottle to the table. He took a healthy swig and said, "Yes, I can see a dog would do that if he loved his master that much that he would spin in circles so as not to offend his master."

The thin man looked confused. "But you had no dog you said so why would it spin in circles?"

Fabre and the larger man looked at each and burst-out in uncontrollable laughter.

"See, man... you do have humor behind those eyes!"

24 Janvier 1942 - 06:00 Heures

In the distance, the bells of *Notre Dame* rang six times and a pounding on the hatch door of *La barge de Matteo* stirred the larger man from a sound sleep. He smacked his lips together with a taste of a herd of dead animals in his mouth.

"What? What is it?" he said in a delirious voice.

"Frenchie, fire your boat. You work today," said the German soldier.

"What? What is it you say?"

"Get up you lazy bastard. I say you work today!"

Matteo, the larger man, looked around his galley and saw Fabre had stripped the fur off the woman and placed it over the thin man who had collapsed on the tiny cot next to the woman. Fabre went to the opposite cot and lifted the hatch to its storage locker and pulled out several coils of rope, cans of motor oil and old rags. He lifted the woman from the cot and placed her into the long slender box and he placed his Sten gun on top of her. He then re-arranged the bedding as Matteo had left it.

Matteo pulled the pin of the locking clasp and slid the hatch open. The sun had not broken the sky as yet but he still squinted in the pre-dawn light.

"The blizzard has ended and the day will be bright," said the German soldier. "Wake your mate. We shove off at 6:15."

"Right... all right! But let me piss in the pot first," said Matteo. Annoyed, he closed the hatch with a *thud*.

"Will he come down here?" asked Fabre.

"Maybe, but not usually. I have coffee and cigarettes in the wheelhouse. He'll go there first and make the coffee and smoke my cigarettes."

"He comes with you?"

"Yes. You know us French can't be trusted," he said jokingly.

"Let the thin man sleep. I'll take his place."

"You know the skill of a barge master?"

"I know the skill of a fisherman and I will learn the skill of a barge master. The science is not remarkable." said Fabre.

"Very well, it is your head. What is your name so that I may call you by name?"

"Fabre. Call me Fabre."

"Okay. I tell you man as being a barge-master is not remarkable, do the spring line first, the one that is diagonal and coil it on the dock fast. Do the bow line next and throw it onto the bow and coil it after we make way. Do the same with the aft line. When we dock, throw the bow line first to the dockhand and I will bring the barge around to the dock and then you throw the aft line to the guy. You understand?"

"Yes, I understand. And what do I call you?"

"Matteo. My name is Matteo."

Matteo bent and raised a pot to the bench and unbuttoned his trousers and began to piss in the pot.

"Ahhh, the first piss of the day always feels good, don't you think, Fabre?"

"My piss is bound in nerves. Maybe later," he said.

Matteo grabbed the steaming pot and opened the hatch and tossed its contents over the side into the Seine.

"You a better man now, Frenchie," said the German soldier sarcastically with a cigarette hanging from his mouth.

"*Heer* Hans, you know my routine, why do you interrogate me so?" said Matteo in a hearty laugh mocking the German soldier.

"Because Frenchie, you need discipline," said Hans, the German soldier.

"Ha, from you? All you do is drink my coffee and smoke my cigarettes. Here, give an old man a hand out of this blessed hole."

The soldier stepped to Matteo and held out his hand to help Matteo step out into the frigid air. Fabre looked up and saw the German soldier and as soon as the soldier saw Fabre he raised his rifle to him.

"Who is this man, Frenchie?"

"Ay, that's only Fabre. He used to run these waters before you thugs came to Paris."

The soldier watched Fabre, his frame sturdy and strong. He watched closely as the unknown man came out of the galley to the deck.

"We are now thugs are we, Frenchie? And what of you? When is the last time you took a bath? You stink."

"A pleasurable bath was before you invaded us. Now I can't get time to have someone wash me because you thugs take all the time with our washer women. You've exploited them and now I can't afford them."

Hans, the German soldier looked at Matteo and said, "You should get a better job then, Frenchie."

"Who then would have coffee for you and cigarettes for you to smoke?" Matteo looked over to Fabre who had been standing on the deck taking in the exchange between the German and Matteo. "Quickly Fabre, do your work so we can leave this place."

Fabre leapt from the barge onto the dock and untied the spring line and coiled it quickly with several wraps. He then charged the bow line with the same enthusiasm and tossed it onto the bow of the barge. Matteo had entered the wheelhouse and cranked the cold motor.

"Come on, bitch." He cranked her again and the engine sputtered to a run. "That's my bitch... good girl you are. The stern line!" yelled Matteo to the waiting Fabre who then tossed the line and jumped on board. They puttered away from the dock.

"Here is today's map," said the German. "Don't blow us up." He paused and then said, "Where is your mate?"

"Sleeping. Too much wine last night. We didn't think we would be making a run today."

"Ay, there was much trouble last night at the Majestic."

"Really? What happened?"

"Résistance set a bomb..." The soldier looked at Fabre from the wheelhouse who was coiling the aft line. "...you have known him long?"

"We go back years. Off and on I see him at the dock... sometimes at the coast. He likes fishing more than barge work now. You should talk to him about fishing. He likes talking about fishing."

"I don't like the ocean. I don't like this barge but if I had to make a choice, it would be this barge for I can see land, and on the ocean... I cannot see land."

"Ay, you're a landlubber German."

"Maybe... my stomach does not like the up and down and side to side."

"Ha-ha, Hans, my dear German, then don't talk to the helper or you might get the rumbles of your stomach because he talks all about the sea rolling and heaving and all about his fishing and tales of whales swamping his boat and of his men being thrown from side to side and the sea heaving and waves... and more waves crashing like you just told me."

The soldier quickly left the wheelhouse and his stomach emptied over the side. Fabre looked at him grabbing onto the rail and then up to the wheelhouse where Matteo was clearly laughing out loud. Fabre thought it would be of good gesture to give the soldier a hand so as not to have him interrogate him on any matters.

"Are you all right, *Heer* soldier? Can I give you a hand?"

"No! No, get away from me. Don't talk to me about your fishing... stay away!" The soldier heaved again.

Fabre entered the wheelhouse where Matteo was still laughing.

"What has happened to him?"

"It seems our dear *Heer Führer* dislikes the ocean and fishing altogether. I think I possibly saved you from any interrogation."

"You laugh boldly in front of him."

"The German? Hans is an okay guy for a German. He is only doing what he is ordered to do. He has a wife and small boy in some small village in the mountains. He has traveled with us many times and I would rather have him than someone else of more disciplined manner."

"Will he be sympathetic to our cause?"

"*Our*... cause? No, man, *your* cause. How can one say what goes on in a German's mind? Other than drinking my coffee and smoking my cigarettes, he has not asked for anything. He does not interfere with the loading of supplies nor abuse his authority over us. But to persuade him to look the other way may be beyond what he can do. Who can say... this German's mind?"

"If it comes to that, it wouldn't be pleasant. I have my duty as well..."

"Frenchie, I need bread for my stomach!" yelled the German.

"*Jésus Christ*, I better get down there," said Fabre.

"Hold your place, man. Wait to see what he does," said Matteo.

The soldier slid the hatch open and waved his hand in front of him as to divert the stale smell of air as he descended out of sight. He looked around and saw a heel of bread on the thin table with several empty wine bottles and three finger-oiled glasses with red rings solidified in their bottoms. A stifle of a snore turned his gaze to the thin man who was covered in a fur coat. He bent to the coat and picked it up. On the collar it had traces of red. He opened it further and on the inside were more traces of red entering the sleeves. He looked at the thin man snoring and saw no traces of red on him. He quickly drew the coat under his arm and went up the four steps to the deck. He marched to the wheelhouse and holding it up in his fist, he said, "What is this?"

"A fur coat," said Matteo casually.

"Yes I can see that... but where did you get it and who does it belong to?"

"It is mine," said Fabre. "I took it from a friend, a prostitute the other night to keep me warm after she threw up all over my jacket. I told her I would return the next day with her coat but here we are on the barge and I have no way of giving it back to her."

"What is this red on the collar and inside?"

"Like I said, she is a friend and she had gotten drunk and apparently her man of the evening wanted her coat and not pay her. They had a fight in the alley and I happened to come by and saw my friend fighting for her life, so I jumped in and punched the man's lights out. He had cut her with his knife and after her adrenalin stopped flowing... well she heaved all over me... much like you talking about the sea."

"Stop it!" the soldier said. "Was he German?"

"No, a roughie from the sea. I could tell by his smell as that of dead fish."

"Stop it, I tell you. No more fish or sea stories! Here, take your coat and get it out of my sight."

Fabre took the coat and headed to the galley and as he bent to open the hatch, the FN pistol fell from its pocket. Bending quickly, Fabre recovered it with his free hand before it hit the deck. He looked up at the wheelhouse and neither man was watching.

"Eat my bread, Hans. It will make you feel better and I won't allow this man to talk of his sea and fish stories to you."

"Thank you, Matteo, I appreciate your concern. I don't know how a man can go out there and fish all day long and do nothing and have nothing to talk about, only about fish who cannot talk back. It must be a lonely life. What say you, Matteo?"

"I thought we were not to talk about the sea and fish stories, Hans?"

"Yes, you are right, but I was talking about the man, not his stories. How does one communicate in life if he has no other words to say? He interests me not nor his stories."

Matteo smiled to himself as he knew Fabre would be safe from any questions coming from the German. "Where's that map, *Heer Führer*?" he asked.

"What!...? You have not been watching?"

"Your retching distracted me. OH... hang on, Hans..." Matteo turned sharply to the right and the slow moving barge waddled in that direction, and then Matteo turned his wheel many times to the left. "...Phew! That was close." He looked over to the German who was hanging onto a grab rail and he smiled to himself once again as the German's hands were white.

Fabre had taken the four stairs down to the galley and went to the locker beneath Matteo's bed and he opened the lid. The woman lay there — motionless. He closed the lid and went over to the thin man.

"Wake up, man." He shook him. "Wake up, man."

The thin man grunted and then his eyes opened wide like he had seen a ghost. He sat straight up and hit his head on the bulkhead. He flopped back down holding onto his forehead.

"Why did you startle me so?" asked the thin man.

"We are moving and the German is with us. Do not mention the girl; he knows not of her or where she hides."

"Okay with me." He swung his legs over the cot. "Who are you?"

"A friend... Fabre from last night. We had wine and bread and cheese... and more wine."

"Oh yes. Where is your dog?"

The thin man than looked behind him on the cot and jumped up looking back at the cot where he pointed to where the woman had lain motionless and he said nothing, just pointed to the spot from where he just stood from. Fabre put his finger to his lips and he said nothing.

Fabre exited from the galley onto the deck and moments later a pot came out of the hatch and a warm steamy liquid flew over the side into the Seine. The soldier looked at Fabre who was straightening twisted cargo lines and neatly arranged them in long strips and then turned them in a loop and led the lead to the opposite side of the barge.

"See, I tell you Matteo," said Hans. "...the man has no conversation about him. He plays with the rope and talks to the rope as he talks to his fish and he answers his dialogue as a person speaking to another. I cannot imagine a life so lonely as to talk to rope."

"His boat has less rope than this barge so maybe he talks to the nets as he has more nets than we do," said Matteo.

"He is a poor man that talks to himself and no other — but he must be a good man since he risked his life for his friend who had a knife threaten her life and he had none only his fists to defend her. Yes, he must be a good man — but a poor man."

"Yes, Hans, from what I know of him, he is a good man and he will help a friend even if he knows not this friend but was asked by another to defend this friend. He is a good man."

"There were many lives taken last night by men of no conscience who interrupted a musical whose guest singer was the famous Fräulein Marta Savant. With a professional bomb from beneath the floor caused some men to wander in the streets injured with no purpose while others whined with injustice. I believe if that man would have wandered by, he would have helped."

"I believe he would carry in his arms as he is a poor man of conversation, one who he could save because he would not possess the imagination to help with conversation and determine the extent of injury."

"Yes, Matteo, your description is probably right. Hush, he comes close to us and we need not reassure this man of his poorness."

"Matteo!" yelled Fabre over the whine of the engine. "Shall we lash the containers down with a net before we string the binders as we do in fishing?"

"I have not enough nets. We will only use the binders, Fabre."

"Very well."

"See, Matteo... he speaks of what he knows... nets and fish and the sea. He is a poor man of conversation."

"You are very observant, Hans. They should make you a General."

"If I could, I would try... but I don't have the will to stand judgment over others or the ability to pretend I have such ability. I am a farmer by trade as was my father and his father before that. The land speaks to me as does the wind and the rain so I may choose the right time to plant and to harvest. My wife calls me gifted with this charm of the land."

Matteo said nothing as he thought maybe the German was like this unknown man that pretended to be a barge master and was possibly a fisherman as the man had said, but the fisherman story was the imagination of Matteo and not of this man. If the German knew of this fabrication, would he then think the man was still a poor man? If he knew this man, this strong man, this dangerous man, this smart man who came to him in the middle of the night with a woman draped over his shoulder and that woman was the woman the Nazis were looking for... would he then think the man was a poor man of conversation?

Matteo smiled to himself and kept a close eye on the map.

24 Janvier 1942 - 15:20 Heures

The natural course of the Seine and its accessibility to the North Channel Sea deeply concerned the Nazis with their ability to protect their assets from saboteurs. Daily, they would maneuver a series of mines on the Seine's west branch and catalogue each placement for the safe passage of movement of ammunitions.

By mid-day, just outside of the southeastern Paris boundary, the daily map indicated that the mines were intermittently spread and finally disappeared altogether. *La barge de Matteo* and its precious cargo labored at a leisurely speed — more of a putter — to forty kilometers south of Paris, past *Melun*, and then another three kilometers took them to a hamlet with a small train depot called *Brolles*. Its access to water and rail and vice-a-versa allowed for supplies to be shipped inland to where the Third Reich's troops and equipment would support the drive through France. It was here in the hamlet of *Brolles*, to the southeast, where Fabre thought he would rendez-vous with the Résistance at *La Forêt de Fontainebleau*. If he could escape the eye of the partisans and any German soldiers that might be hosteled in the small barracks, logistically, he thought, he would be able to secure safe passage down to Vichy where the new government of France had formed. The farther south he travelled, the safer he felt.

Fabre had noticed, once they secured the barge, that the snow had been piled high from clearing the tracks and two buildings occupied this particular stop. One was a hostel that housed the Germans, and the other, a small freight office.

The loading of the barge was a painful sight, thought Fabre. Pallets were dismantled and their wares of fruit, vegetables and meat were then re-assembled on the barge. He thought a container-type system would greatly increase the speed and add to the security of the products brought on board. He imagined a wooden structure that could be raised by a crane and then lowered into a support system to hold it in place would eliminate the need for heavy ropes. He then saw a Medic vehicle being driven onto the barge with a cube-type container where the injured were placed and immediately in his progression of thinking, an idea completely erased his former thought. A metal container — one which could be stacked on top of each other and held in place by a series of pre-welded stakes, would simplify the matter even more.

By the time the Nazi soldiers and dock hands loaded the barge, it was already getting too late to return to Paris. Another night of discomfort with the German and the Nazi guards did not taste well with Fabre. He licked his dry lips. This would be his only chance to get the woman off of the barge and hidden in the forest... but how? From the unoccupied wheelhouse, Fabre scanned the dock and observed the goings-on of the dock hands, the guards, the German and Matteo and the thin man. He could easily have stuffed this woman known to the Germans as 'Marta Savant' into a sea-bag and thrown her over his shoulder and carry her off — but not under watchful eyes. Fabre hollered down to Matteo, "Captain Matteo, shall we disembark all the soiled rags and raunchy garbage to the burn pile over by the trees?"

"Good idea, Fabre." He waved his hand to acknowledge Fabre's wishes and then turned to the thin man.

"Retrieve the shit wagon over there by the shack and bring it to Fabre to load with all of our debris."

"What?" said Léon, the thin man, with a questionable look on his face.

"Do as I say and with no further remarks. Bring the shit wagon to Fabre so he might load it."

Léon trudged over to where a wheelbarrow-type cart with large bicycle tires on the rear and smaller ones on the front sat empty, tilted up on its edge draining from the last liquid of its bearing. He wondered why Matteo ordered him to bring such a thing to the man called Fabre. They had no waste of any significance that one could not as easily be placed in a bucket, but to drag this burden through the snow was a task of utter uselessness. Begrudgingly, he flipped the cart to its wheels and began the task of endurance leveling the snow with the imprint of the bottom of the cart and its skinny dual lines of tracks. He crossed the train tracks and waited for the dockhands as they secured the medical van and then proceeded as the Captain ordered. Past the wheelhouse he pulled and to the back where Fabre waited.

"Thank you, Léon. I meant no struggle for you as I could have very well retrieved this cart myself."

"Do as you must, I shan't help you no further," said Léon. And he left.

The sun sat caressing the distant tree tops and the clouds once again started to roll in with their darkness. Only a few lamps were lit on the dock and the Nazis were getting anxious and hungry. The cold bit through them and they rubbed and breathed into their hands, their breath rising and vanishing. It was Fabre's time to make his move. Down the steps to the galley he went to the slim locker and pushed aside the bedding and the fur coat that now resided on the floor. He opened the lid. His precious cargo lay as he had left her and her breathing was shallow and short. He reached for her fur coat and wrapped the fur around her and gathered her into his arms and carried her through the hatch and placed her gently into the cart.

He rushed back down into the galley and gathered old rags, ends of chafed rope, which had been cut off of well-maintained line, old newspapers, and his Sten gun. Fabre placed the gun on top of her and then spread the newspapers about her and stacked the rope and old oily rags on top of them to disguise his precious burden.

Fabre pushed the cart through the maze of laden to the ramp where the authorities gathered. As Fabre passed, one of the authorities lit a cigarette with a match and with the flame still burning he tossed it into the shit wagon. Fabre reached out with his gloved hand and like a first baseman, he caught the flame and snuffed it out in his fist.

"Oily rags *mon wachtmeister*," he said with a smile and continued to push the cart off the ramp, across the train tracks and followed the trail that the thin man had made and beyond. The Nazi looked at Matteo, who just shrugged his shoulders, and nothing more was made of it. The Nazi and Matteo turned their backs to the direction of the increasing wind and from the direction of Fabre. A heavier dusting of snow was now beginning to fall.

18:15 Heures

The sun had fallen past the treetops and the spears of light rays had disappeared. The rolling clouds now covered the sky and the blackness opened up upon them as the white crystals fell heavier, coating the dock in a fresh layer of white. The last pallet had been disassembled and its product was being tracked to the barge by the dock hands and re-assembled on the barge's pallet. Men hustled back and forth trying to beat the incoming accumulation of snow. Fabre's tracks were dusting over and his figure was but a speck as he neared the fire at the edge of the forest.

A figure with a pitched-fork stood at the edge of the fire, stoking it with stabs of steel, and cinders floated in the air at each stabbing lighting the sky with orange buds snapping and disappearing into the blackness. Fabre approached who appeared to be an old woman wrapped in a patch-worked coat and scarf wrapping her head and the ends tied in front. She looked up at him. Her green eyes sparkled.

"*Bonsoir Monsieur*," she said. "You are not German by your looks. Who might you be?"

"A friend of the forest," Fabre said. "I have debris from the barge and a burden of frail nature that must be held safe. Can you help me this night and I will be off before the sun rises?"

"Bring the cart to the edge around me to my right. Any view from the barge is blocked by their hostel," she said, her voice muffled behind the scarf.

Fabre wheeled the cart to where the old woman had said and they both gathered the debris and threw it upon the fire. The oily rags withered like a snake twisting and turning and puffed and lay as the rest and hardened-like and when poked by the pitched-fork turned to ash. She gathered the papers and rolled them, then twisted their ends like a giant hand-rolled cigarette and tossed them into the fire. Within a brief moment, they flamed and then turned to ash. The old woman looked into the bottom of the cart and saw the frail burden and she then looked at the man in the orange of the light and his face was kind and his eyes were of concern. The men of the dock were out of sight and she bent to the frailness and touched her cheek with tenderness.

"Take her to just beyond the edge of the trees. I will return the cart to the shack as I always do and you must be out of sight! Lay low and I'll return to you."

"*Merci*," said Fabre. He bent and gathered the woman and picked her up into his strong arms and he stepped through the snow with his frail burden and went beyond the edge of the trees. The old woman tilted the cart to its back wheels and pulled it behind her through the calf-high snow to the edge of the shack — like she always did. The wind was strong and she could smell the smells from the chimney of the hostel as the stench traveled in waves in the night's air. As the noise and laughter and singing erupted from the hostel, she knew, the Germans were in for the night.

The old woman returned to Fabre and his burden. She led the way, bent to the wind, down a cleared cart road until they trudged deeper into the forest. She turned to the forest and the wind diminished and they were able to walk together between the trees — straight and erect. The weighted snow behind them continued to fall and the wind that had been a hindrance now covered their existence from where they had walked. She held the Sten gun with the strap over her shoulder that Fabre had given her to carry. Together without words they trampled through. As they came upon a small lake in the center of the forest, the woman turned to Fabre and said, "Four more kilometers until we reach a farmhouse at the hamlet of *Chailly En Biére*. There is a stone fence and at the end is a row of tenement. There we will find a *cachette*."

"At the end of the row houses we find a safe house?"

"*Oui*," said the old woman. "We rest here. I go and break ice at edge for water. Do you need water?"

"Yes, water would be welcomed, merci," said Fabre. He licked his dry lips. Fabre laid the woman down and put his ear to her mouth and he felt the air go in and come out slow and shallow. He put his hand on her forehead and she felt warm to his cold hands, maybe even hot as his arms themselves were trembling from the strain and his touch was uncertain. The old

59

woman rejoined the two and she knelt beside them and she offered a cup of water to the man. She bent as well and listened to the young woman's breathing and felt the woman's forehead. She looked at Fabre.

"She is very warm. She needs a doctor."

"Do you know of any at the safe house?"

"Maybe one that we can trust. The others live in fear, and I don't trust a man who lives in fear. He who lives in fear is not trustworthy and will do strange things out of fear. But there is one I trust. I will send word to him."

Fabre forced a smile and thanked the old woman for her kindness and for her help and for the chance to save this woman she did not know. Fabre brushed the flakes from his burden's face and covered her face with his scarf and then gathered her in his arms and lifted her up – he stood tall. The old woman guided them through the forest, their path lit only by the snow and by her intuition. They came to a clearing and the old woman stopped and told Fabre to wait for her to cross and if it was safe, she would signal him to follow. He watched her cross the clearing knee-high now in snow. She walked proud and she walked steady, one step as strong as the other, straight as an arrow, a compass not straighter than how she walked. She landed at another tree line and Fabre could see her wave her arms and he began to walk and he walked in her footprints. They reached a path and then farther down that path they found a stone wall and beyond that stone wall, Fabre saw a row of row-houses. They walked to the end and they turned at the end to face a stone cottage with a pitched roof. A gaged, yellow light filtered out spilling onto the snow with long shadows casted between its bars. The old woman stepped onto the porch and dusted her patch-worked coat and removed her scarf and turned the knob of the door and held it open as Fabre carried his burden through the door. She entered behind him. The fire was warm. She grabbed a pillow from a chair with ease and placed it on the couch and told Fabre to lay the woman down.

"Charlie, *mon père*, come, get dressed and go get the doctor who we can trust." A thin, frail man stood at the doorway to his bedroom with a shotgun in his hand that he could barely lift. "*Ma fille, quoi*?"

"Go get the doctor we can trust. This woman is in need of a trusting doctor. Hurry old man, she is not well!"

"If you tell me how to find him, perhaps I should go?" said Fabre.

"My father can go. It is good exercise for him. Besides the doctor might not come for you and he might put up a defense if others observe your presence. Get dressed old man and get help, say it is for me, I'm not well."

The old woman went through a doorway, out-of-sight of Fabre, to her honey-oak ice chest in the kitchen and chipped a cube of ice off and brought it back to the young woman. She bent to her and began to run the ice along the young woman's lips. "How long has she been like this?"

"One day at approximately this time."

The old woman unbuttoned the young woman's fur coat and opened it to find her dressed in workmen's clothes. "You did this?"

"*Oui!* Her dress was torn beyond mending. What you see was the only clothing we could find."

"Clothes of a coalman and she dresses in fur. You might stand back when she awakes to find herself dressed in these and not in clothier of fine women's apparel." The old woman looked at the young woman's hands. "And nails finely polished and manicured will no doubt find your flesh beneath them if you stand too close," said the old woman with a hint of humor.

"It was not my intent to humiliate her but she was awarded to me at the wish of a dying man. I could not leave her in her state for others to admire and then abuse her with interrogation. It would not have been just and no justice would have been served to be humiliated in those conditions," said Fabre.

"Ay, you are a man of conscience but one of bad taste," said the old woman followed by a burst of laughter. With a more serious tone the old woman said, "Is she of wounds since you have admired her in her nakedness?"

"Admire was not the case but I noticed she is well made and no not that I noticed or saw, madam."

"You take life too serious, man. I play with you as she is a very lovely girl for a man of your stature and character no doubt."

"You toy with me why? I made sacrifices to save her as this was my duty from the lips of another man."

"One you killed?"

"No, not I... Well not directly. I had no hand in shooting her suitor."

"But you do realize that her suitor had to be a German officer for her to be styled as she is?"

"I claim nothing, and it is of no concern."

"Well maybe you should think again, man, as the SS are looking for your charge and will stop at nothing to find her. You do know who she is, do you not?"

"I've heard rumors. And how does an old woman who shovels shit and places debris upon a fire and stokes that fire know of such things?"

"So that is who you think I am because you saw me for ten minutes doing as you described?"

"I wish not to discredit your worth; I simply state the concern I have for the safety of this woman before you."

"Well, Monsieur Gage Fabre, I know enough to know who you are and what you have done, which was a great endeavor for our country and England, which I commend you for your bravery. But Monsieur Fabre, you interrupted me in finishing my job of blowing up the rail station and that barge on which you found solace."

Footsteps and voices could be heard outside getting closer. Fabre grabbed his Sten gun and poised himself behind the door just as the knob turned. The old man and the doctor stepped inside.

"Marie-Madeleine," said the doctor. "What... or should I say... who have you rescued now?"

The door closed behind them and the two men turned to see another man holding a Sten gun and looking like he was about to be overcome with grief.

"You... you are Marie-Madeleine?" Fabre said slow and apologetically. "You are the leader of our Alliance?"

"Don't sound so surprised that I could be the one as you say. It matters not. What matters is that we need to move this woman as soon as we can. Doctor, what do you say?"

"Well, Madeleine, let me examine her first." The doctor looked up at Madeleine, and then turned to the man holding the gun.

"Nothing he hasn't seen before, doctor. Her modesty is not in question," said Madeleine who then removed her wig and stripped off her padded body. "Phew, that feels better," she said as she stood there as young and fit as Fabre. He stood in amazement. But he had already put *deux et deux* together. Her statement of blowing up the train station, knowing his name and his mission and now her name confirmed by the doctor could only add up to one person. Fabre felt proud to be in her presence.

"We need to get her to Vichy and she needs to be healthy to tell us what she knows of the Germans' plans for the rockets. Fabre I need you to go back to the barge and seek out the thin man, Léon. You will help him to finish in setting the charges and then my comrade you must go back to Paris. I will take the woman with me. She will be safe, I promise. Take this bag and give these timers to Léon. Now go Fabre, the way we came before you are missed in the morning."

Fabre looked at Madeleine and then back at the young woman who lay on the couch.

"What is her name? Her real name?" he asked.

"We know her as Marta Savant. She has been instrumental in gathering us intelligence on the V-Is project.

She risked her life and now you have saved it. God and France be with you, Fabre."

Fabre gathered his things and looked once again at the woman lying on the couch and the doctor that now attended to her and to the woman who he admired and he nodded with respect and opened the door. He stepped out.

He trudged along in the snow retracing the steps that they had taken, alone and again to the wishes of another, and he knew he must now help the thin man, the man Fabre thought was still-in-the-mind. Was he the engineer of destruction?

In the empty field, the one where Madeleine had him wait, the wind had picked up and it blew with force and the snow whipped at him. He had seen wrongly and accused wrongly in mere perception and yet again with the thin man, he had wrongly set in station that did not define the man.

He had learned a lesson and would not assume again.

25 Janvier 1942 - 03:15 Heures

The fire at the edge of the forest lay in smoldering ashes still warm and crackling with annoyance, sending its orange glitter upward. They snapped in the blackness and disappeared. Fabre edged out past the burn pile to the cover of the freight house to where he could smell the smells of the hostel, and the quietness stilled the night. He moved to the shit wagon and crouched behind it and peered in both directions for any movement. When he felt safe from any threat, he moved from the shit wagon and headed towards the tracks and the loaded barge.

What would Fabre's answer be if questioned of his whereabouts by the German, Hans, if he had remained on the barge with Matteo? If provoked, Fabre would have to kill him. But then what of the morning when they must depart? Crouched next to the barge, Fabre thought of the words spoken by Marie-Madeleine that he had interrupted her from blowing up the train depot and the barge. He shuddered with the underlining possibilities, but he now was faced with a duty to finish what Marie-Madeleine had started. As far as the German was concerned, he would take his chances and maybe make up a story of his fishing.

Fabre stepped on board without detection and edged his way to the entrance of the galley to the drawn hatch. He knocked as he did before but heard no voices. He slid open the hatch. He peered in.

"Where have you been, man? We need to go," said the thin man, Léon, holding a Sten gun poised at the open hatch. Two men lay in silence on either side of the long thin table.

Léon grabbed a small black bag off the table and tossed his Sten gun through the opened hatch to Fabre. "It is all set in here," he said coldly. "Did Madeleine give you the other timers?"

"Yes," said Fabre.

"Good. We have to set the timers under the hostel and on the track. The dynamite is in place. I assume since you made it back from Madeleine's, you are a man I can trust otherwise you would not be here," he said.

"I am as surprised as you," said Fabre in a joking manner. "My dog needed to have a piss."

"Ah ha, you make fun of me when I drink. I have not the blubber of a whale to hold my wine as you and that thief, Matteo. He had his last drink and also that Kraut. They are no friends of mine — either one. I spit on them. They know what they know and they know what terror our families are going through and yet as they know, they do nothing to help but gave in to a dictator, a madman. And we are supposed to crawl like weak animals, like snails in the grass to bend from our heritage because he says so. No! I spit on them. And I spit on those who know and who do nothing and those who crave the *franc* like Matteo and those who support Fascism, and those who want to kill our French way."

Fabre thought the thin man had some issues that might take a long time to discover but he knew Léon spoke the truth. At that moment, in Fabre's mind, he knew of what Léon asked. Fabre was well healed on the task at hand and he would do as instructed for the good of his country.

They crept to where the barge had been set with the ramp that no longer held it in place. The gunwale had been raised and bolted, and they crept to this spot to take watch and to observe the hostel. "The train will be here in forty-two minutes and then they will all be awake and moving about. We need to place these last two timers and then run like hell," said Léon.

"Where do we set these timers?" asked Fabre.

"One goes under the hostel and the other across the tracks to the ditch... where the switcher is located. Since I am of smaller frame, I will take the hostel as to slip under easier than you. You take the switcher. There are only two wires, a black that goes to black and the red that goes with the other. Attach them as I say and then pull up on the alarm's plunger. It is already set."

"We are to head to Paris after this mission," said Fabre.

"Yes, I know. We will hook up with the underground there if we make it. Shhh... Some Nazis are already aroused; I can hear them so be careful."

"I got it, Léon. I will meet you down the tracks."

Léon and Fabre, one and then the other, slithered over the gunwale and each took their way. Léon scrambled to the hostel and went to the back and dug like a dog through the snow and then slipped under the hostel just as one of the guards stepped out. He was late—they were late. The guard rounded the front of the hostel on the north side — the side facing down the tracks and to Paris. The guard unbuttoned his trousers and a long stream of piss soaked the snowbank and its collective warm liquid ran creating a crevice beneath the hostel and headed for the stack of dynamite. Léon tried to gather more snow and place it in front of the stream to divert it but the snow was too light under the hostel and the liquid pooled at the base of one of the sticks. He prayed the acid of the piss did not soak the paper barrier and cause an early explosion or worse, flatten its might and turn it into worthless mush. Léon hooked up the timer, pulled up the plunger and waited. Two more soldiers stepped from the hostel and in turn, unbuttoned their trousers and relieved themselves against the snowbank as the first. Léon could not move for risk of being heard and then shot. They would then discover the dynamite and the plan would be lost.

Fabre was deep in the reeds of the river before the water's edge, moving at a snail's pace, observing the soldiers as they started to gather outside of the hostel. There was only a half hour left before the explosion and even less for the train to arrive. He had to pick up his pace. Fifty meters seemed like fifty kilometers as his fingers dug into the snow groveling in servitude to get closer.

Léon watched the legs of soldiers step from the hostel and some turned to where the ramp had been. They noticed that no smoke came from the smoke-stack. They also noticed that no one stirred and the engine of the barge was quiet. Two spoke together as observed by Fabre and then an officer came to them and they spoke of the idleness of the engine and lack of movement on board the barge. The officer conveyed an order to them and each split from the other and where the ramp would have been on either side of that they crouched with their rifles pointing onto the barge. The officer called for two more soldiers and they stepped onto the barge surrounding the inventory, and stepped quietly from each to the next, crouched and expectant. The officer joined his two soldiers on board and he made way to his superior position in the barge's wheelhouse. He scanned intensely over the tracks and to the burn pile, to the freight building and back to the other side of the wheelhouse.

Fabre laid flat and did not move. He felt his body temperature rise as he lay still — adrenaline pumping, and again at the oppression of a German. Fabre had to move. He had to reach the switcher, and he felt the ground trembling and heard a not-so-far-off blast of the train's whistle. The officer turned at the sound and looked down the track in the direction of the approaching train. Fabre made his move. Forty meters, thirty meters, twenty meters and then he dove behind a tree and looked back. He saw the smoke of the train's engine stack above the distant tree line.

He pushed off from the tree. Ten more meters to go. His mind raced. He thought about getting shot in the back and not being able to hook up the timer, and he thought of the woman he had carried and how he had braved the blizzard, and how *she* had braved the blizzard. He thought of the old woman who was not old, but as young as he. He reached the switcher. He plunked down beside it where two bare wires poked out of the snow like two tiny eyes. *Black to black and red to the other*, he repeated in his mind. He twisted the wires together and pulled up the alarm plunger and placed the timer beneath a timber. He then covered it with snow.

Fabre laid his head down on the other side of the switcher to the rail and sighted down the track. He could see the engine of the train round the last bend and its catcher displayed the snow that had gathered on the tracks whirling a white wave of violent turbulence. He felt the rumble in his stomach. He saw the thin man lying flat under the hostel – still, and he knew the thin man knew. Fabre slid down the bank to the reeds. Through the reeds he ran, one foot cresting the water's edge, the other planted like a goat on the steep bank. There was no looking back now, only forward.

Fabre heard the train screeching to a stop, metal-on-metal, and imagined the sparks flying as he did not look back. He heard the steam escaping with a resounding *hiss*. And then, as moments idled, he heard the inexplicable resonance that cracks your ears and forces your body to tense in fear.

He gasped for air as he moved his heavy frame through the weighted snow and he heard the creaking of steel as the train lifted from the tracks. Again, the thunderous crack—the barge exploded! Timber was strewn skyward with all of its cargo. The turbulence whipped in the air. Split boards wacked at the fruits sending them out into the Seine and as far as the burn pile. And as the debris fell, Fabre heard the water *sizzling*. He imagined the screams that he had heard before and he imagined Léon, the thin man, smiling as the plunger hit its mark and he knew Léon knew.

Fabre dove into the snow and lay still with his face down and his arms and legs spread. He lay there breathing as the clamor behind him continued and the debris continued to hail down, wood splintering and the *swishing* of water washed over the snow-covered banks. The clatter started to settle and Fabre rolled over onto his back and only looked to the sky. The *hissing* sound of melted snow touching hot metal and the smell of burnt flesh wafted in the air. Fabre rolled onto his stomach and steadied himself as he stood to his feet.

He trudged towards Paris through the weighted snow and he never looked back.

10:00 Heures

Madeleine and her friend were traveling down the back roads, the blanket of white hiding the stakes of the grape fields and the perception of the road's width. The depth of its drainage ditches were also lost and joined as one. Only the feel of the old, rutted road beneath kept them true. They headed for Vichy in a medic van with the woman known to them as Marta Savant. She lay still in the back strapped to a cart. The doctor, Madeleine's friend, told them that the woman had a concussion and without proper care she could fall into a deeper coma and never return. Madeleine sat with the woman and watched her as they rolled through the countryside on their four hundred kilometer journey south. She raised her eyes from the woman and looked out the two small windows of the back doors and saw the sun rising in the sky. She felt a shiver within her and she returned her stare to the woman who lay with no emotion — still. She appeared to be lost in her mind's thoughts, ricocheting images crossed and merged — all muddled.

Madeleine imagined the two men had finished their mission of blowing up the train and hostel and she hoped they were on their way to Paris. Her mind played past scenarios and her adrenaline spiked and her fingers entwined in nervous retrospect. She eyed once more the two small windows and drew a deep breath. She wouldn't have news until after they had arrived at Vichy — but still she felt the anxiousness. And she felt pride.

22:17 Heures

Fabre's steps were heavy. His journey down to Brolles had been easy on the barge with idle conversation and as the German looked at him, he felt his stares and said nothing — a muttering perhaps from beneath his breath but words of no consequence. He hadn't slept since the morning before last and he was tired from carrying that woman. He was saddened with the thought of Léon but he knew that the thin man knew. He thought of the woman, Marta Savant, and he thought thoughts that he shouldn't think — but he thought those thoughts as they propelled him farther forward.

He took a handful of snow and pressed it to his lips and he swished it in his mouth and turned it into liquid. He gratefully swallowed. His mind talked to him in riddles, and he, back to his thoughts. His pace slowed and he tired now. In his delirium he thought he would lie in the snow and rest out of the wind. He would rest, he thought, out of the wind. A spot to rest — out of the wind — where he could rest. His muscles ached. They were not listening to him as he trudged through the snow to find that spot where he might rest.

Ahead he saw a barn and then another that looked like the first and then the latter joined with the former — and then they were one and then two again. He walked in the blinding snow towards them and then they were one as he opened the door that the wind demanded closed. He pressed his body against the barn and he pried the door open and the air felt warm as he stepped inside. The wind blew closed the door behind him. He looked around and he found a spot out of the wind.

He collapsed on the hay in the empty barn.

26 Janvier 1942 - 16:00 Heures

The sun had come up and it had hovered at noon and by the time the late afternoon had arrived, the town of Vichy was cast in long shadows of oranges and reds. The medical van had stopped, and men and women dressed with red and white arm bands had rushed from the warmth of their hut out into the wind. They gathered the woman who was strapped to the cart and brought her into the warmth of the hut and placed her upon a bed of cotton-wrapped feathers. Her head was propped with a pillow and an intravenous drip was set up beside her. Her clothes of a coalman were cut away and removed and she was washed and inspected for broken bones. A chair was brought in and Madeleine sat and watched the woman. She watched with sadness in her heart as this eighteen year old lay motionless. It was understood that she had slipped into a deep coma and now — she was in the hands of God. Whatever sacrament that had kept the coma at bay had faded away.

Madeleine stood and bent to her and kissed her on her lips. She gently touched Marta's cheek, then Madeleine stood tall and she turned to face the nurse who stood at the foot of Marta's bed. The nurse gave Madeleine a hopeful smile and then she took the chair beside Marta Savant's bed.

"Please," said Madeleine, "...keep me informed of her condition. The doctor here will know how to reach me. Keep her safe, kind Sister." Madeleine turned and left the two in the disappearing light of the day.

Walking in her bombardier jacket, fleeced-lined trousers bunched into her high boots, and with scarf wrapped around her neck and one more turn around her head covering her face from the harsh wind, Madeleine braved the weather and headed for the telegraph office. She entered through the door and went past the teller to the back room where she met a man, her friend whom she could trust. After entering a *salle de concierge* and closing the door behind them, they went to the back wall where they released a small lever and shifted a rack of cleaning supplies to the side. They removed a hidden panel and went through. They paused briefly on the inner landing to reinsert the panel and to manually turn a crank which slid the rack back in place tight against the back wall of the closet. The two went down the ladder to the room below.

Several lamps were lit, and each placed on several tables. Large wooden boxes sat on the dirt floor and shelves scattered with smaller boxes, some of tin and some of wood with racks of rifles lining the walls. On one table spread taut were maps and upon those maps, red X's marked through smaller black circles but there were many more black circles than red X's. On the other table were a stack of identification passbooks with forged Nazi clearance documents folded into them. Also on the table was a local newspaper, freshly printed with an article circled referencing multiple explosions that rocked a town along La Seine. BROLLES was highlighted with bold letters across the top of the four-column wide photograph.

"Here," said the man, "...the article reads of many dead Germans and several Frenchmen. It says that the remains of one were found in the center of where the German hostel would have sat."

"And the other Frenchmen?"

"Only one other. He was found floating in the river."

"So, one got away. Do we know yet which one, Victor?"

"No one has shown up in Paris."

Victor was a man of five feet ten inches with dark curly hair and a moustache, and bright blue eyes. He was naturally tanned from toiling in the grape fields his entire life. His hands were strong and he walked with a slight limp from an accident as a child when he fell out of a tree at his grandfather's estate — but his disability had never held him back.

"We should not assume the worst," he said. "Either man is capable of finding refuge if they are injured. Léon is wiry and his instincts and motivation are strong; he will do well to find help. The other, Fabre, is strong and smart and he has that charisma that could charm the boots off a German for a pack of fags. Either one will do well."

"Yes, Victor I know you are right and that is why these two men were chosen. But it was I that sent one of them to their death. I need to know which one so I may pray for forgiveness."

"Forgiveness, *mais non!* You have no right to claim forgiveness for they knew the circumstance. They knew and you know they knew. They knew what they must do. We did not bring this upon ourselves... the Germans did. It is they who need to pray for forgiveness from our almighty God... our French God," said Victor with fire in his eyes. "As you told me once, we leave self-pity on the dirt floor and we put rifles into our hands and the hands of our brothers and the hands of our sisters to force these animals back to their own country. Do you not remember telling me so?"

Madeleine raised her head from staring at the newspaper article. She looked into Victor's eyes. "Yes, Victor, I remember well... and I remember watching them kill my father and your father like they were criminals, thieves of the worst kind or as rapists or child molesters. I remember saying that to you, Victor."

"Well then, Madeleine, we must use all of the grenades in this room... and all of these bullets in this room must pass through the bellies of these men... and all this dynamite must tear down their hypocrisy," said Victor as he lunged to each to emphasis his spoken word.

She smiled and placed her hand on his chest, "You should become a statesman, my dear friend and leave the grapes for men of lesser stature."

"I will if you join me."

Madeleine shied away and then looked back at the man who as a young boy had climbed a difficult tree because she had dared him. "We need to gather these weapons and load the medical van. Our comrades are waiting and in this snow it is a good day's drive to Paris."

He smiled at her and said, "No injury lasts forever unless it is one of the heart, Madeleine... and my heart is full and strong."

. . .

Fabre awoke to the sun beating through a steepled window that perched out from the pitch of the roof. And next to the window were little elephants, giraffes, lions, zebras and funny short men cut-outs pasted on the white walls. The sheets smelt of lemon and as he lifted these sheets, he was naked beneath them. He checked his chest with his hands and raised his hands to his eyes and rubbed his eyes and thought he must be alive and that this room was not a dream. A tiny knock tapped on the door and he panicked looking side to side for his weapons and found none and he lifted the sheets again and he saw his nakedness and...

"Monsieur," said a sweet, muffled voice. "Are you awake? I have your clean clothes for you. I will leave them outside the door so as not to embarrass you. Are you awake, Monsieur?"

"Ah, *oui*," he said. "*Je vous remercie!*"

"Lunch is being served downstairs in the kitchen."

"Thank you, mademoiselle. I shall be right down," said Fabre.

Fabre pushed the sheets aside and tip-toed to the door and gently turned the knob. He stuck out his hand to feel for his clothes. He heard a giggle and quickly dragged his clothes into the room and closed the door. He dressed quicker than he had ever before; even his brow had sweet-beads forming. He pulled on his thick wool socks and looked around and saw nothing more of his things. He opened the door and stepped to the landing and looked down. A pretty girl maybe twelve years of age was standing at the bottom and was shyly looking up at him. And then she disappeared into the adjoining room. *Well, they're not going to whack my head off in clean clothes*, he thought. *And certainly not in front of children.*

He descended the stairs and turned left at the bottom following the direction of the young girl. At the doorway, he stood still and looked at the well-dressed table where two women of his approximate age, the young girl that he had seen, an older man with a long beard and a man of middle age sat, staring back at him. The long array of windows allowed the brightened room to appear — heavenly.

"Come in," said the older gentleman. "Please sit with us."

Fabre walked to where the gentleman had pointed, which was on the opposite side of the table as the two women of his age, but next to the young girl. Each gentleman sat at either end of the table. He thought one of the women looked like another from his imagination and she looked at him and smiled, but she did not speak.

"We thought you would have slept another wasted day away," said the older man.

"Grandpa," said one of the two women, "it was not his choice to collapse... of exhaustion, I presume. Only a man of dire straits would attempt such a feat in this weather. And being a strong man as he appears, he should not lie in waste."

Fabre was offered bread and stew and a glass of wine.

"I have no recollection of my walking into your home last night," said Fabre.

"Last night? No, my young friend, this is day *three* that you slept like Sleeping Beauty," said the older man.

"Like whom?" said Fabre.

"Ay, I see you are a man of nil children," said the middle aged man. "A French fairy tale later collected by the German brothers Grimm and published along with Snow White and the Seven Dwarfs and others."

"I know not of what you speak, sir," said Fabre.

"It matters not, young man."

"I can show him the book, Great Grandpa," said the young girl.

"I don't think a man of his intent wants to read children's fairy tales, my little one."

"If I hear right, I have been sleeping for three days?"

"Tonight would make three. My sister found you in the barn," said the talkative one of the two older women, "...when she was gathering eggs."

"Where am I?"

"A small place called *Évry*."

"How far from Paris?"

"About six hours as the crow flies in good weather. A little longer in this terrible white stuff," said the grandfather.

"How long walking?"

"That is walking. In a vehicle, less than an hour."

"So I am very close then," said Fabre with a smile on his face. He took a mouth full of stew and broke bread placing some in the stew and more into his mouth.

"If you don't slow down young man, the bread will strangle you and we will have to cut you up and feed you to the pigs."

"Grandpa, that's not nice. He is a strong man that needs his nourishment."

"He eats like my horse," said the grandfather.

"He just needs the right woman to teach him etiquette," said the talkative one.

"Rose, that will be enough. I imagine our young friend will want to get on the road and join up with his friends. He appears to have gained his strength and a will to move on," said the grandfather.

"Ah yes, that is correct, sir. I mean not to impose on your hospitality any further. If you could direct me to my things, I think I should be going."

"In the barn, under the haystack. My son will show you."

Fabre took the wine and swallowed it all and said his good-byes. He looked twice at the one who had gathered the eggs and who had found him, the one that didn't speak. The middle-aged man showed him to the barn and Fabre followed. In the white they walked, and into the white barn they passed and to where his weapons lay.

"My father speaks harsh to stir one's thoughts, pay him no mind. I tell you one on one. Go to where the *Bastille* stood and take the underground — and be careful. There is a ticket agent with a patch over his eye. Tell him you have friends in *Évry,* he will take you to another tunnel and he will give you a ticket to go on where you can join up with others. Hang on, my friend. The ticket only he can give."

"I know not of this man but will do as you say. And excuse me, sir, but your daughter, the one that does not speak, the one that found me, have I met her?" asked Fabre.

"I have but one daughter, the one who spoke to you. Take care young man and be safe. Our future depends on strong young men like you," said the middle-aged man.

"I shall try. And thank you for your hospitality."

Fabre stepped into the white.

29 Janvier 1942 - 07:15 Heures

Madeleine and Victor had stayed one more night in Vichy and headed out the next morning early as the sun broke and the cocks began to crow. It would take them all day and maybe into the night to reach Paris, and that depended on whether or not they would have to avoid German patrols the closer that they approached Paris.

It had been slow going for everyone and they heard the rumble of heavy equipment from over the hills clearing the roads so the German infantry could travel. Madeleine and Victor stayed to the smaller country roads away from the main roads and as far away from the Germans as they deemed necessary and still make Paris within a reasonable time.

The empty fields passed them by and the sparse empty farmhouses stood still as the owners had escaped to Spain, while others had packed up their belongings and had gone to England. Victor carefully maneuvered the medical van as Madeleine kept a watchful eye scanning the countryside for any possible trouble.

The afternoon was upon them and Madeleine thought of the young woman, Marta Savant, who had been saved from the rubble of the Majestic Hotel. She also thought of how the man called Fabre had risked his life to save her and how he had carried the woman in his arms when most men would

87

have not carried on. That was over three days ago and no word had been sent of Fabre or Léon's return to Paris.

She looked over the fields and back to Victor, her life-long friend who cared for her deeply and she knew that he cared and she cared for him but now was not the time. She had hatred in her heart and she would ask no man to share in what she must do. Taking her gaze away from Victor, she looked again out her side window. Madeleine thought she saw something in the open field and shouted, "Stop, Victor! Stop the van!"

Victor slammed on the brakes and the van slid to a stop. Madeleine anxiously rowed down the window. Her breath rose in the cold air.

"What is it, Madeleine? What do you see?"

"I don't know, back there a bit. Go in reverse until I say stop."

Victor put the van in reverse and backed over the ruts he had just made. Again she said, "Stop! Look over there." She pointed to a brown spot in the field. "Do you see it?"

"*Oui,* it looks like a cow's back."

"There are no cows out in this weather, Victor. Come, let's see what it is."

"Madeleine, we should not stop for idle curiosity. We need to push on."

Madeleine did not heed his words and she stepped out of the van with her Sten gun wrapped around her neck. Victor followed as he did and then they split to approach whatever it was from opposite angles to the object. As they neared, Madeleine knew. She rushed the brown bulk and all the while as she trudged through the snow, she cried out, "Fabre! Fabre! Fabre!"

Victor arrived first and grabbed the man and turned him over. His face was covered in ice crystals and blisters. They gathered him up and the two struggled to carry the limp Fabre through the knee-high snow to the van. Madeleine opened the back door and Victor bent over to let Fabre fall upon him. With a hefty heave from Victor and a forearm push from Madeleine, they were able to get Fabre into the van.

The delirious Fabre said faintly, "Beauty... sleeps."

26 Février 1942 - 10:30 Heures

The catacombs of Paris twisted and split, and twisted and split again. Only one who knew the markings could find that particular catacomb where life could be restored, and it was where Madeleine and Victor had brought Fabre.

Fabre lay in his bed, two-arm distance from the next, with Manuka honey salve on his face and on his fingertips. His hands and face were bandaged to keep the dust of the catacombs from entering. He had been found weak but alive and now after a month of healing, he was showing signs of his masculine self. And on this day, as every day, Madeleine and Victor had come again to witness his recovery.

Fabre sat up-right and was with patience as the doctor started to un-wrap Fabre's bandages from his hands. He then began the slow process of removing the bandages from Fabre's face. Down to the last wrap, the doctor was careful in his removal and then the last wrap pulled evenly and neatly from Fabre's face. The doctor cautioned him to open his eyes slowly as the light of the day that he was about to see was the dim light of the catacombs and not to be concerned of the dimness. His sight would be blurred, but the doctor hoped not for long.

Fabre did as the doctor said and at the foot of his bed stood Madeleine and Victor. And to his right, the doctor stood bent over to Fabre and peered down at him. The sheets smelt fresh with lemon for this was the first he had noticed. He batted his eyelids to the dimness of the caged bulb that hung on the ceiling of the catacomb. His eyes became slowly accustomed to the light. Fabre looked up. He saw the one-eyed doctor with patch over his eye staring back at him. Fabre raised his hands to his chest, and then he felt his eyes and stroked his face. He thought he must be alive and this room was not a dream. He looked around and to his left a young girl of maybe twelve of age sat on her bed reading a fairy tale.

Madeleine cupped her face with her hands to hide her tears. She looked at the strong man, Fabre, the kind man who had saved a woman and carried her for many kilometers in his arms — the man the Résistance could be proud. But as she looked at him his expression was like a lost soul who had miraculously come back to life.

"Where am I?" he asked calmly.

"In Paris, in the catacombs under the old *Bastille*," said the doctor. "Let me examine your eyes..." He shone a light and continued to say, "...good, very good. And how does one see?"

"I see... I see a farmhouse, a white farmhouse. A farmhouse with white walls and funny things and animals stuck to the walls and a family of two women and a young girl and an old man and his son sitting at the table. The one didn't speak, the one who found me but she looked at me and smiled and they fed me and told me to come here and seek you out," said Fabre.

"Where was this farmhouse that you speak of, Fabre?" asked Madeleine.

"I don't know. I was blinded by the snow and the wind," he said.

"Fabre, please believe me as I tell you the truth, man. Madeleine and I found you in a field and there were no farmhouses around... only barren land. And, you looked like you had been there for days. Maybe after you made the explosions at the dock and train station..."

"But they fed me wine and bread and stew," Fabre reasserted.

"Do you remember what you said when we picked you up and placed you into the medical van?" asked Madeleine.

"No."

"You uttered the words 'Beauty... sleeps'," said Madeleine.

"And what is that? No, wait, I remember! It is a child's fairy tale..." He looked over to the young girl who had a book in her hand and the title he saw in his mind was in German and he spoke it out loud, "...*Kinder und Hausmärchen*."

Madeleine looked at Victor who in turned looked at the doctor.

"It is possible in battle fatigue that a soldier experiences things that we doctors and science cannot conceive."

"What do you mean?" said Fabre who was getting a little annoyed.

"The good doctor is saying that you might have thought you talked to these people but they do not exist, if and only in your mind. And the book you described is the first book the Brothers Grimm published in 1812," said Madeleine.

"How would I know this? I have never heard of these brothers before. And the agent with the eye patch, I was to see him for he had a ticket for me so I could carry on and meet up with the rest of the Résistance. I knew this, they told me to hang on," said Fabre.

"Yes, Fabre," said Madeleine. "It was the angels telling you to hang on, no one else, *mon amis*."

"The girl, the one that did not speak, she looked akin to the woman I carried in my arms. It could have been her and her family?"

"I am afraid not, Fabre. She only came out of her coma the other day. It has been over a month that she has lain there still," said Victor.

"My God, what has happened to me? Is my mind at last ends that I smelt the freshness of the sheets and the taste of their food and the swallow of wine that warmed my stomach and all the while I was face down in the snow like a dead animal?"

"You have been blessed by the angels, my friend. Others would not have survived in that blizzard as you did," said the doctor. "I have no other explanation for you medically or scientifically other than theologically."

Fabre lifted the sheets. "Where are my clothes?"

"There is a voucher on your side table that you can hand to the nurse who will fetch them for you. We had them washed as you had no need as you were," said the doctor.

Fabre looked into the faces of his comrades. His mind swirled like an endless tape, only stopping at a moment of recall, and then replaced as quickly by another.

25 Mars 1942 - 14:00 Heures

The whitewashed room, bright and puritan, impersonated a state of holiness with its painted furnishings tolerant of the iron bed that sat sideways to a high-arched Baroque sun-soaked window. It opened to the street below — *Boulevard Carnot*. Above the third floor room's hand-carved doorway, a wooden cross with a bronze cast image of a Jesus hung in respect.

When Marta Savant first awoke, she imagined she was in heaven. And as she had looked around, the sterile surroundings added a dimension of shock to her. There was no emotion, joyful or not, nor was it pretty, but she was thankful. It had been a month since she had regained consciousness and as she had passed her hands over her protruding stomach, she felt the bane of injustice that now grew inside her. She remembered feeling rather melancholy as she sat staring out the window on her welcoming clean white sheets, stretched tight. She struggled with remembering her savior, his image lost in her subconscious and his words, if any, were indiscernible words — but she had felt a presence, a presence of warmth and a heartbeat. A strong heartbeat.

What she thought she had remembered was a dream-like nightmare, and the one who had stripped her of her innocence was faceless. And as the *Gringoire* newspaper and rumors from her immediate-care circle had declared — perhaps her suitor was German and an SS officer.

The nursing staff had given her a cameo found within her belongings — in an inner pocket of her fur coat. She now held it in her hand, her index finger tracing the outline of the embedded ivory face. She flipped it over and noticed an inscription: 'M – *meine Liebe – sei sicher* – SSBFMVW'. Marta read the inscription, *my love — be safe*. She felt no connection as she fondled the piece but for some reason, she felt ashamed and didn't know why. And as her comrades had told her of her sacrifice and of her contribution she had made to the Résistance, it had no bearing on her. For those who knew of Marta, and for her protection, they called her by a different name — Clarissa. Marta was also instructed to say, if questioned, that the father of her child, a Frenchman, was killed in one of the British bombing raids and therefore was not at her side. And Marta was told all this by a woman named, Marie-Madeleine who had held her tight and then rushed from her sight.

One night, after Marta had become more aware of her situation and after trying to understand her predicament, she had uttered these words in silence: *What am I to do with this baby that grows out of discourse? But as I feel it grow inside of me, I concede that it is also part of me. I cannot bear the shame of such deliverance and what of the patriots? Would they not chastise me and would they not do the same to this child who has no bearing of defense?*

Those words spoke to her again this day as she let her mind wander as she looked out the window.

Sister Bernadette dressed in a white apron and winged bonnet with an outfit striped in robin's-egg blue, knocked lightly and then stepped into Marta's room with a congenial smile and a tray of delights. Marta looked up and smiled.

"Mademoiselle Clarissa, thé et biscuit?"

"How thoughtful, thank you."

The Sister eased the tea and cookies down to a small table beside the iron bed. "You seem to be of stronger mind today."

"I am gathering my strength because of your kind attention."

"It is good for the baby to have a strong mother in the mind. You are its tree and your child shall be the fruit. I'll be

97

on my way and I will see you at tonight's prayers before our evening meal."

"Yes, thank you, Sister Bernadette."

After the Sister left, Marta stood up from the bed and slowly walked to the larger table that supported a mirror. She rested her hands on the chair in front of the table and looked at her reflection. As her hands felt the backstay of the chair and her eyes met the mirror, a seemingly jolt of lightning jarred her with an image from the past. She quickly stepped back and looked at her hands and studied them and then back to the chair. Once again she placed her hands upon it. This time, there was no other jolt of consciousness — but an image played out in her mind. Marta remembered. It was all clear like a newsreel playing in her mind and she remembered the shouting and the music and the red dress and as she turned she remembered the look on that man's face as he rushed from behind a curtain. And then... she could not remember anymore. Marta looked down and touched her bulging stomach. She remembered she had no stomach until she awoke in her bed in the white room.

This is what they talk about, she thought. The Sisters had talked to her as if she knew what they talked about because she was awake, but until now she was confused with what they had said. Not until this jolt had she started to see clearly.

But why do they call me Clarissa? Surely, they must know who I am? Maybe not? Maybe the Sisters have no idea and the woman who talked to me has said my name as so? I must find this woman. She must have the answers. And with every bit of strength in my body, I shall not have this baby on French soil! she thought to herself.

. . .

Mother Superior stood at the side of the small altar beside an ornately-carved podium dated from the time the residence had first been built, 1794, four years after the beginning of the French revolution and *La Constitution Civile Du Clergé*. It managed to remain unscathed through the February Revolution of 1848 and the First World War of 1914 and to this date. The convent had served its community, sometimes secretly, with its spiritual needs and its physical needs. Mother Superior was the sixteenth in its long history to govern her flock.

Closing the evening prayers, Mother Superior said, "May thee Lord be with you and guide you through these times as He has in the past. Go in peace."

"Amen," responded the cloistered nuns finalizing the ritual with the sign of the cross. The Sisters stood and as everyone was set to leave the chapel and head to dinner, Marta approached Sister Bernadette.

"Good evening, Sister, as I am feeling much better, I am inquiring whether you would be able to share a pen and paper so I might write down my experiences."

"Let me see what I can find, my child."

"Thank you, Sister."

"Come, let us dine."

The room, down the hall from the chapel and into the other wing, was sparse without décor other than two long tables divided by rows of chairs on each side with a walkway down the middle. This space also substituted for a playroom on Saturdays for the children of the village during course weather and now a meeting place where friends of the forest could gather in privacy. Sister Bernadette had excused herself after dinner and as coffee and biscuits were served, she returned with a leather bound journal dressed with a clasp and a small Cryptex lock. She handed it to 'Clarissa' with a smile.

"Oh, no, Sister Bernadette, I cannot accept this. It is too elaborate for my intentions. I mean, it is so beautiful with the leather carvings and fancy lock."

"Nonsense, my child. I have no use for it." A sparse group of engaged Sisters prepared to clear the evening meal. A systematic chore, rich in tradition gave way to a private audience between Sister Bernadette and Marta.

"It was given to me a few years ago by my aunt who thought that since I was entering into my flowering years, I could capture my growth from child to womanhood. As you can see by the blank pages, I have not experienced enough to enter such words. My uncle, who is a historian of ancient antiquities and a bit of a collector of intricate locks, made this journal for me. He said it holds secrets, which at the time, made no sense since the pages were empty. Please, take it as yours so you can recount to your family of all you have been through. I am sure you can fill half the pages even at such a young age." Reaching out, the Sister touched Marta's stomach. "Maybe if you write your experience down, it will give closure to your anger and you will allow God back into your heart. I might have done the same but my embarrassment would not allow me and I turned from my family and devoted my life to God."

"I am sorry, Sister. I had no idea of your sorrow."

"It is not for all to hear. I have made amends with myself and only wish you may do it sooner than I."

"May I ask, Sister... where is your uncle who made this intricate lock?"

"The Nazis took him to evaluate their art acquisitions that they had stolen from Egypt. The last I heard, he was still there at one of the tombs transcribing hieroglyphics of supposedly an ancient map of magical waters."

"That sounds intriguing, Sister."

"Not according to my aunt. My uncle lives in fear."

Marta held her new journal to her heart and said, "I shall treasure this gift forever."

10 Juin 1942 - 09:00 Heures

Marta's treasured journal that Sister Bernadette gave her never left her side. She had set to memory the unique cryptic combination that her friend had shared with her. It made the days seem shorter as she scribed the events as much as she could remember. And as Marta grew in strength, she was able to take morning walks and she enjoyed so very much the fresh air with all of its fragrances.

Word had been whispered throughout the convent that because of the attack on *SS-Obergruppenführer* Richard Heydrich in Prague on May 27th, 1942, by the Résistance, and his ultimate death on June 4th, on this day, June 10th, 1942, by the order of Adolf Hitler and *SS-Reichsführer* Heinrich Himmler, the town of *Lidice, Czechoslovakia* was brutally destroyed. Mass shootings of the male population over the age of fifteen years were carried out. The women and younger children were gathered up and taken to a death camp. This news angered and saddened Marta, so much so, that she wanted to rip out the annoyance within her and join with others to fight these hideous monsters.

Marta, however, was a planner and as such she had solicited the help of one of the Sisters at the convent in brushing up on her German. Marta was a natural with languages. The town of her birth, *Tournai*, Belgium, bordered France and Germany. It had been mandatory to study these languages throughout her primary and secondary school classes. She had also grasped the nuances of the English language to broaden her future skills. Even though the Nazis had just occupied France, Marta, at sixteen and a half years old and in her direct approach, challenged the board of Directors of the most prestigious medical school in Paris. Her grades and enthusiasm won them over and Marta moved to Paris to begin her education in the medical field. Maybe not a smart move considering the Nazis' presence.

It was there, in Paris, as she fed long neck birds floating in the ponds under the gaze of the Eiffel Tower that she had been approached and recruited.

Marta's life forever changed.

17 Août 1942 - 09:30 Heures

Marta had made an entry in her journal and had jotted this date down as being very special as it was the first time for an all-American bombing raid on Europe. Also, her pregnancy was getting to be more than she could bear and she felt it was time to leave the convent and head towards the German border. Marta had fully recovered from her injuries, but not from the injustice that protruded from her belly. Her determination remained strong, which motivated her to charge forward with her promise.

Madeleine had made arrangements for Marta to ride in the back of a Medic van that was going to take Marta to *Lyon,* France under the guise that she needed intense pre-natal observation. There was a driver and two female nurses. Their actual mission after they dropped Marta off was to haul back a shipment of arms that was being flown in from Switzerland. It took the pseudo-medical team four and a half hours, mainly traveling through back roads, to go 175 km. Not fast but consistent. Marta was informed that when they arrived in Lyon her safest route in her condition would be through the train station, *Gare de Genève-Cornavin* in Switzerland, and not to embark on the train from Lyon as too many Résistance sympathizers were being rounded up by the *Malice.* Marta was also advised to stay with the roadway and if the possibility arose to hitch a ride with a produce truck to take her to *Genève*, Switzerland. These routes had been well established to fulfill the needs of the German officers who were on furlough.

Through an acquaintance of one of the nurses, Marta was quickly introduced to a middle-aged man, Dante, who — despite his objections — took pity on this young woman's situation, and the two of them made the long drive to

Genève. Idle chatter occupied most of the trip but during one of their conversations, Dante asked, "You are so young to be married, with child, and now a widow?"

"The war has not been kind as you are well aware. Things happen sometimes that you have no control. The death of my husband was one of such occurrences."

"Where are you headed after Genève?"

"My husband has family in *Bern,* Switzerland. They have agreed to watch over me and help take care of their grandchild." A story perhaps, but trust wasn't given out lightly.

"That is very kind of them. You are fortunate to have such a family. Times are harsh even for families to stretch their resources farther. Yes, it is not as rare anymore to see families take in complete strangers."

"You have experienced this?"

"I tell you as you are a friend of a friend that we all need to join together to stop these atrocities. I feel a spirit within you and although you say what you said, I believe you hold a greater adventure than one you say."

"What are you saying, Dante? Speak without riddles."

"I have heard of one, young and determined who gave their life. Their code name amongst the Résistance is the *'La Cygne'.*"

"The Swan?" said Marta.

"Yes. If, by grace of God, this person is alive, I would swear my allegiance to one so strong, no matter what age or gender."

"And where would you find this person, if they exist?"

"I would come once a week, on a Friday, to this very station and wait until such a person presented themself."

"Would that not be a waste of time if one didn't show?"

"I have faith. There have been many instances of unlikely patriots, contrary to belief that have risen to defend our French culture." Dante looked back through his rear window for traffic and then pulled to the side of the plaza's walkway.

"You are a good man, Dante. If I hear of the one you speak, I shall instruct them to meet you here. Good-bye, Dante and thank you."

"Never say good-bye... it's too final. I prefer, until we meet again. Mademoiselle, you have not told me your name."

Marta smiled and closed the door of the van. The two had travelled for three days together and not once had Dante asked this burning question. It was the 20th of August 1942, when they arrived at the entrance of Gare de Genève-Cornavin. He had dropped Marta off and smiled back at her as she closed the door in silence. Dante looked up at the three-floor high building that was built in 1858 and he knew he would be back and he believed he would meet this woman again. Dante, as a young boy had witnessed the twelve year remodel of the station after the establishment of the League of Nations in 1919. And as a man, he still remembered his father's history lessons regarding this marvelous work of engineering.

. . .

Marta had found a café to buy a small lunch and sat at a cast iron table and watched people and soldiers come and go. Although Switzerland proclaimed their neutrality, it was apparent the SS officers strolling along without a care, had no interest in hiding who they were or where they were. She was nervous one might spot her and then arrest her. But not wearing her usual glamorous make-up as she did on stage, and returning to her natural blonde hair, she appeared more modest. Her protruding stomach also might have offered some sort of immunity.

The train departed at 22:46 from Gare de Genève-Cornavin. It chugged alongside *Lac Léman* (Lake Genève) and along its path, while offering spectacular views of the snow-covered Alps. It stopped at every hamlet to just past the town of *Lausanne* on the north side of the lake. From there, it steamed to the foot of *Mont Pèlerin* where a northerly climb led to the Swiss-German border. By the time the train reached Bern, Switzerland, Marta felt the kicking was definitely intensifying. Caressing her stomach she muttered to herself, *This... what is inside me has to be a male. It kicks like it is doing 'der Strechschritt'.*

The slow moving train from Gare de Genève-Cornavin finally terminated in *Olten,* Switzerland where Marta had to disembark and seek another train to take her to *Lörrach*, Germany. She had selected this quiet town because of its location of being out of harm's way and she had heard the hospital was well situated for birthing mothers and had a sensibility to the French.

The extreme pains that Marta felt carried with her for almost a week. If she wasn't so stubborn, she might have stayed in Bern. But, on 2 *Septembre*, it was either the news that Rommel had been driven back by the British Commander, Bernard Montgomery in Africa that excited her or the rattle of an earthquake that rocked the valley. Whichever, Marta cried tears of joy as she looked up into that bright globe. She was glad this intrusion that was taking over her body was coming to an end.

The nurses, although sympathetic, had questioned her on her decision for putting the child up for adoption so soon. Marta would not apologize for her decision, it stood as it was. The child was German as far as she was concerned, being born in Germany of a German soldier. Before Marta released the infant, she wrapped his leg with the brooch that was given to her by the SS tank commander so that maybe one day the boy may use whatever means to know his heritage as a product of the Third Reich.

Two days later, Marta left for Genève.

11 Novembre 1942 0 12:00 Heures

Marta made an entry in her journal:

The provincial government of Vichy was overthrown by the German-Italian military sweep, code name: Fall Anton. The last directive of the French navy before dissolution on 27 Novembre 1942 was the scuttling of the French fleet in *Toulon*. Three battleships, seven cruisers, twenty-eight destroyers and twenty submarines were set ablaze denying Hitler of their might.

A strategic force in the Mediterranean was now a twisted pile of rusting steel.

23 Avril 1943 - 18:00 Heures

Fabre's whereabouts from the time of his discharge from the catacombs of Paris had been spent blowing up bridges and rail lines to discourage the Nazis' moral and movement of precious cargo. He rallied in the quick, commando strikes — hit the mark, disappear, and then gather for the next one. There was no time to sit around for days discussing strategies. He took pleasure in the chaos he created. His ambitious nature had not gone unnoticed by the Résistance and now he sat with a couple of fellow comrades on the precipice of his most challenging mission.

Paris, *Avril* 43' appeared far more lively, even with its fresh dumping of snow as it rebounded from a harsh winter and Nazi rule. Sheltered in place in the servant quarters on the sixth floor of a friend's apartment in the 8th *arrondissement,* Fabre peered through the yellow-stained curtains, past the curved window to the street below, 8

Avenue de Messine and to where a hub of six streets including *Boulevard Haussmann* came together. As he and two others sat in the rotunda, their position clearly gave way to view the main route from the Gestapo's headquarters at 11 *rue des Saussaies* to 84 *avenue Foch*, the home of their main counterintelligence, known as *Sicherheitsdienst*. The view from the alcove window had allowed Fabre to spy downward, watching, scribing his notes, calculating and, at times, relapsing to his dream, his frozen memories that seemed so real. A jarring noise from a truck's bouncing cargo after hitting a stubborn-iced rut would regain his focus.

The street was clear, looking to the westward and southward directions. A telegraph office situated across the street employed a sympathetic collaborator, Fabre's cousin's schoolmate, Bernard. He was due to come out of the telegraph office for a smoke break. It was 18:03 as Fabre eyed his pocket watch and the 18:10 train was about to arrive at *Le Gare Saint Lazare*. A wire had been received by Bernard and he in turn sent the station master of Le Gare Saint Lazare an 'all clear'. Bernard appeared through the door and took out his cigarette package of *Gitanes.* He first offered one to the German soldier on guard duty. The guard cupped his hands to concentrate the flame from the flip-top lighter and took a deep inhale.

"You a good guy, Bernard. *Danke*."

The air was fresh enough to crystalize his warm breath upon his exhale. Bernard didn't say a word. He took two drags and tossed the fag down, and then he ground it into the sidewalk. Fabre looked intensely as Bernard's shoe pointed inwards. Bernard went back inside to the warmth.

Fabre turned away in frustration. They would all have to wait for tomorrow. Behind him he heard, "Fabre... any news?"

"*Non*... not tonight." Fabre went to his cot and sat down, removed his boots and swung his legs up. He then placed his hands behind his head and looked up at the chandelier. *Goddamn, what is holding those guys up? They should have been at the switching station by now.*

His thought pattern was broken by another Résistance team member, François, who picked up a chair and carefully moved it to where Fabre was lying and set it down. "I know you get frustrated, Fabre, but we have to wait. We have no choice. The plan will not work unless the train is stopped."

François went to the small, alcove kitchen and picked up a pot of coffee and two mugs. He returned to where Fabre was lying on his cot. François sat down in his chair.

Fabre continued to look up at the chandelier. He was a doer, he hated waiting for anybody. "Yes, François, you are right. I know. I know how I get. I should have gone with them."

"You are needed here... for the plan. We cannot lose you when we have others willing to die for the cause."

"That is my concern. I should have been the one. I have defied death before and I will do it again. To send such young boys to do a man's job is not right."

"Were you not young like these boys? We all here have defied death's grip. Our next mission," François paused as he recounted a near-death scenario, "...we might not be so lucky."

François handed Fabre a mug and poured coffee into it and they watched and they calculated and schemed as they hid behind those yellow-stained curtains.

The 8th arrondissement of Paris was the most ruthless and dangerous area of all of Paris. The Gestapo and French Malice would harass men and women for no reason other than for their own enjoyment. Fabre was taking a great risk to gather intelligence, and transfer that information to SOE couriers who would then send radio messages back to England.

Le Gare Saint Lazare was situated one kilometer from Fabre, in the 8th arrondissement and was one of the largest and oldest train stations in France. If not already famous enough, Claude Monet had made several impressionist paintings in 1877 honoring its presence.

The train from *Saint Lazare* to the coastal town of *Le Havre,* France was an important route for the Nazis. Along this passage, the Résistance had witnessed the loading and distribution of long range missiles, the V-1s — which, according to information, had the capability of reaching England. Prototypes had been fired off and hit targets in Belgium, the Netherlands, and along the coast of France where the occupation had strategic footholds.

All of a sudden, a disturbing *scraping* down at the entrance of their building had set Fabre and François in motion. They had an escape route planned if need be. A dumb-waiter that serviced the six floors had been upgraded with the addition of a couple of heavier cables to withstand several men and their weapons. Everything else would have to be left where it was.

François listened closely at their door and motioned to Fabre and to the third man, Jean Luc, who had been resting from doing his morning shift, to not move. Whoever it was, was speaking French — then all went quiet. François opened the door and went to the circular stair balcony and peered over the edge down the open spiral. Two men holding tight to the gold-leafed wallpaper that surrounded the staircase ascended in silence. François motioned to Fabre with two fingers up. Fabre grabbed his Lugar and came to the door in his stocking feet. Removing one of his socks, he wrapped the Lugar's barrel. The two waited intensely while the other, Jean Luc, moved to their escape hatch with their ammunitions.

The intruders' shadows elongated by the windowed landings spread across the floor. One shadow appeared larger than the other. The shadows stopped on the fifth landing lost by the disappearing light at the edge of the ornate trundles. A man looked up to the top floor. François quickly pulled back. The intruders continued making their circular climb as Fabre waited with his finger on the trigger. François stepped back and went inside their apartment, leaving the door ajar just enough for Fabre to peek out. Fabre waited. The intruders finally came into view. Fabre swung the door open and stepped out.

"*Mon Dieu!*" he said softly but emotionally. "Daniel? Alfonso? What are you doing here, man?"

"Mon Oncle!" said Daniel in excitement. The two rushed up the remaining stairs to the top floor. Daniel flew into his uncle's arms. "You're alive!"

Alfonso joined in, arms embraced and hands patted each other's backs. "We had no word to your whereabouts," said Alfonso.

"What are you doing here?" said Fabre.

"Bringing word to those that occupy this apartment. We had no idea you would be here."

"Enough... it can wait. Let me look at you, Daniel. You have grown up," said Fabre. He then turned to Alfonso and said, "Thank you, my friend, for looking after my nephew."

"It was not easy, I tell you. He is a stubborn one. We searched for you for days, in and out as we could without arousing suspicion. No one knew of you or where you had travelled."

"My destinies lead me south of Paris and then a miracle happened, and I wound up here. Please forgive me, this is François, and this is Jean Luc. We have been a team blowing bridges for the last few months. We just returned from the Alps and we are already a week here. Now what news do you have for us?"

"I have my trucks ready and waiting to take the three of you to *Reinickendorf*, a suburb of Berlin, where intelligence, as it might be, has it that an abandoned military ammunition storage site is being used to develop the V-1's. We are to meet up with others of the Résistance as soon as the train to *Le Havre* is stopped at *Vernon*, just before it picks up speed beyond the curves at *Bonnières-sur-Seine*," said Alfonso.

"We have been waiting and wondering. What has taken so long?"

"The Swan is a perfectionist, I am told."

"I've heard the name but don't know who he is," said Fabre.

"A ghost, I heard. It is rumored that they have returned from the dead to save France," said Alfonso.

"A rumor we will no doubt have to verify," laughed Fabre. "But now, come drink with us and we will watch tomorrow for good news from our comrade, Bernard!" Fabre said with excitement upon being re-united with his nephew and old friend. "Come Daniel, take wine with me. We celebrate tonight."

24 Avril 1943 - 18:00 Heures

Fabre and his friend Alfonso peered through the smoke-stained curtains down to and across the street to the telegraph office where the Frenchman, Bernard, stood outside sharing a fag with a German soldier.

"Look down there, Alfonso. Watch the foot of the telegraph operator. He tells us when the train is stopped by the Résistance and then the trucks will pick us up."

"Yes, Fabre, it is my trucks that will pick you up. I have made arrangements to correspond with the train harnessing. They will take us to a *rendez-vous* of which I am not privileged at the moment to know. It is all part of the grand scheme as orchestrated by the Swan."

"You mentioned this person yesterday. What do we know of him? I have met Marie-Madeleine, the *Hérisson* (Hedgehog) when I took that woman down to Vichy, but she made no mention then of this man or when I last spoke to her in the catacombs recovering from delirium."

"I have not met this person either, but am told of a character, much like you, a fearless fighter and dedicated to the cause."

"Well then, my friend, we both shall indulge in satisfaction upon our introduction to such a person."

"And what of that woman, Fabre? Did she survive?"

"She hadn't spoken a word or made any gesture while in my care. However, Marie-Madeleine said that she had come out of her coma only days before me. I have not heard of her recovery or her whereabouts."

"Yes, it was a shame to have watched her lay in such indifference. You are a good man, Fabre. I wished her no ill-will but I could not have stowed her away. As it were, we were interrogated by the SS."

"I understood your dilemma and as you have done to save my nephew, I am in your debt."

"Look now, Fabre! Your man's foot points outward. The train has been sabotaged. You must gather your weapons and head downstairs."

"Ah, at last! My patience was running thin. Now we will set a new front to fight these dogs. Hurry everyone, gather only what is necessary to survive!"

Alfonso gathered what little he brought and said to the others, "Yes, do as Fabre says. We will have supplies in the trucks for the trek north."

The excitement was steaming from their bodies, their faces alive, but as rehearsed, the five men quietly and methodically took each step down the circular staircase in their stocking feet; one hand holding their boots, a pack strapped on their backs, and their Sten guns in their hands.

From the main floor, they diverted past Suites A1 and A2 to where a door led down another staircase to the boiler room. Hidden behind the massive heating system that supported a maze of metal tentacles, they laced up their boots and waited at the cellar's door for sight of Alfonso's trucks. Avenue de Messine was a popular thoroughfare appropriated by the Nazis where one had to employ extreme caution during all hours. At 18:20 hours, ten minutes after receiving word of the sabotaged train, Alfonso's canvas-backed, five-ton trucks rambled to a stop at the cellar's street-side entrance. Four men jumped out of the cabs, two from each and as one from each truck dropped the tailgates, the other two rushed to open the steel panels that resided flat on the sidewalk. An elevator rose from beneath. Hidden by the steel panels, the five men waited for Alfonso's instructions before darting to the waiting cover of the canvas-backed trucks. Alfonso's men knew the procedure. Several oak barrels were rolled out of the trucks to the waiting elevator and as one rolled in and dropped out of sight, another rose with an additional worker rolling and together, they lifted them into the backs of the trucks until all five men were hidden and safe.

Alfonso and Daniel rode as driver and helper in the cab of one truck and Fabre and François took up residence in the other. The cadre of fighters crossed over Avenue de Messine heading east and then one avenue more before they made a left turn, heading north.

. . .

That evening at 20:00 hours precisely, the heavily-disguised Swan was ushered through the door of a basement shelter along with four armed men; two who had stepped to the front and two that lingered behind. Only recognized by punctuality, these newcomers were escorted through the main room, which was occupied by a collection of Résistance fighters. The chatter amongst them hushed as the fighters watched a noble presence being guided to a secured room with a heavy wooden door outlined by black iron plates and steel hinges. There, in the middle of the room, a map was displayed on a table and surrounded by each of the leaders of the associated groups.

The Swan reached out with dagger in hand and pointed to their largest target to date, the research center at *Raketenflugplatz* rocket airfield in a suburb of Berlin. Words were not spoken. An envelope with each leader's code name was dealt around the table in accordance with their strategic implication on the map. Each read and each understood their implication and each knocked the table with assurance. A ceramic bowl was held above the table and each letter was deposited and then set on fire. The swirling smoke rose in a wavering column.

As the mysterious five were about to leave, one of the leaders asked, "Is the information up-to-date?"

One of the five, a man called Dante, turned around and said, "We have men traveling north as we speak, good men, men of strong will and courage. I fear they will be arriving before us. We must hustle to join them and to protect them. The target is heavily guarded and has thousands of slave laborers forced to abide the Nazis' will. Is that not enough but to liberate our fellow countrymen."

"I meant no disrespect; I speak only of the intelligence regarding the manufacturing of the V-1's. I say, only as hearsay, but there might have been a migration to another facility."

"And where did you hear this?" said another voice stepping forward.

"Um...," said the questioning leader, stumbling as he heard a woman's voice. "We found a Polish escapee badly beaten and left to die who had the courage and strength to crawl to safety into a barn and was hiding out. He thought the slave ranks seemed to be thinning."

"When was this?" asked the woman.

"A week ago."

The woman turned to Dante. Together they stepped to the side and whispered amongst themselves.

Dante then said, "We leave tonight. Follow your routes as planned. Even if this rumor is true, it would take more than a week to shut down that facility and transport it elsewhere. If not by rail, then the Nazis must use trucks. We cannot delay any further. Are we in agreement *mes amis*?"

A reverberating sound echoed off of the wooden table.

26 Avril 1943 - 11:30 Heures

The caravan of Alfonso's trucks had been met by two more as they neared the research center at Raketenflugplatz as planned and on time. Holding back along the fringe of the forest, they observed an eerie solitude as wisps of wind-blown snow skated across a barren airfield. As the late afternoon day warmed and the snow turned to rain, the airstrip blackened in a mirror of color from lingering fuel and oil. One more truck was to meet them before they launched an attack. Fabre was uneased by the lack of movement as this could either mean a trap or a complete waste of time.

"We should go in, Alfonso," said Fabre. "One or two of us, no more. If it is a trap, we will know right away and you can plan for it. If the hangar is empty, then a perfect place to stay the night and plan our strategy."

"Your patience is thin, my friend. The Swan had passed orders to remain still until all of us are gathered."

"The Swan is late. Already one hour has passed. We have no communication if he has been captured or not. I understood, as you, the importance of punctuality... the Swan is known for this. Something must have happened. It is up to us. François and I will take the lead. You stay with Daniel and the others and wait for our signal if all is clear."

"Fabre, you are a stubborn man. I will do as you ask, but man, hear me... take no chances unnecessarily. We lost you once."

"You are a true friend, Alfonso. The grey skies will give us good cover." Fabre slid over to where François was sitting. "Come, François. We will split to either side and take to the trees until the fence at each end of the airfield. Bring only one belt of bullets for your Sten gun. If it is a trap, there will be more bullets for our men to survive. If the hangar is empty, we will be re-united with the caravan and our load."

"*Oncle?*"

"Daniel, you stay with Alfonso and do as he says. He brought you here safely and I trust he will do the same now. Come François, let us find the answer."

Fabre separated to the right as François fanned to the left. They stayed low to the ground and moved methodically from tree to tree until they reached the fence. Each set their cutters in motion as if they were being conducted by a maestro waving his wand to a beating measure. Each slithered through the mesh fence and each waited. Fabre then signaled François and they broke into a hunched run to the opposite sides of the hangar. Still nothing stirred. They met in the middle of the large hangar doors in plain view of Alfonso and his men. François removed the padlock and flipped back the clasp. The two slid the hangar door slightly and ducked inside.

A noise behind Alfonso and his anxious men had them quickly turning with their Sten guns pointing at an approaching truck. It slowed to their heightened awareness. Two men from the cab stepped out and three more Résistance fighters dropped down from the canvas-covered stack truck.

"Who is in charge?" demanded Dante.

"I am Alfonso, the proprietor of these trucks."

"Why are you so tense as we approached? Were we not expected?"

"Um... yes, but my friend Fabre and his man François, have taken the challenge upon themselves to answer the question of the hangar."

"And what might that be?" said a woman who was dressed like a man and whose face was covered by a scarf. She looked around and over to the deserted airfield.

"To whether we are to fall into a trap or this is a complete waste of time."

"These are your words?" asked the woman.

Alfonso looked around to his men for support. None came. "Fabre is my friend and a good man, but his patience is thin."

"We had trouble as German Panzer tanks paraded in front of us and sat idle. We had no recourse but to wait undetected until they left," said Dante.

"It matters not," said the angered woman. "The instructions were to wait until we were all gathered — not to risk the mission by lack of patience of one man."

"Look!" said Daniel. "My uncle is waving us in."

"Wait!" said the woman. "How do we know it is still not a trap? The Germans might be holding a gun to his head."

"*Non! Pas par mon oncle*," said Daniel. "He would die before giving us up."

"You are certain, boy?"

"*Oui, Madame*. I have witnessed him saving a complete stranger with no consequence for his own life. It wasn't until two days ago that we finally met up again after months of thinking he was dead."

The woman looked at Dante and then said to Alfonso, "Take three men with you and scout the hangar so that we may know that this young man still holds his uncle in high esteem. Keep one man on the outside so that no harm comes to him and that he may signal us to bring the trucks."

"Ah, yes Madame...?" Alfonso hesitated waiting for a name.

Dante spoke, "This is La Cygne... the Swan."

. . .

Fabre and François had entered the laboratory at the far end of the hangar. Only minimal vials and barren freezers, doors half-opened, empty barrels and discarded test tube stands remained. A chalk board, standing alone, rubbed almost grey from countless brushings and miscellaneous pieces of broken chalk lay about in an inner room. Alfonso walked in with a strange look on his face.

"Yes, my friend," said Fabre. "As I see that look on your face, it is a complete waste of time."

"I thought that as we arrived but said nothing to annoy anyone. My look is not of disgust but of concern."

"Concern? For what? We just need to regroup and find better intelligence. We are lucky that we are all together without any intercourse with the Nazis. We are but a small handful of courageous fighters. Perhaps this guy, the Swan needs to reconsider his motives and allegiances to rectify this misgiving."

"Again, my friend, you are reading my face wrong."

"What riddles are you implying?" said Fabre as he continued his search, moving discarded papers and broken glass with his foot. He was on the opposite side of the chalk board when the Swan entered — unnoticed.

"Where is this man that holds such a high opinion of himself that he disobeyed orders?" the Swan demanded.

Alfonso, who also stood on the other side of the chalk board with Fabre, looked at Fabre with a hint of a smile.

"Well? Where is he?" she continued.

Fabre turned to the direction of the annoyed woman while moving the chalk board slowly with the barrel of his Sten gun. He stared at this figure dressed with a black beret and a scarf around her disguising her face. He looked into her piercing eyes — sharp as a dagger — and said, "And who might you be that is ordering men of courage around like a school mother might to young children?"

"They call me La Cygne," she said with great pride.

Fabre started to laugh. "You are the man... the Swan we hear about." Alfonso rolled his eyes.

"You mock me, sir?"

"I dare not. You should have me write my wrongs many times on this chalkboard."

"You, sir, are an insufferable, arrogant, and tiresome man. You think that your brawn is the only strategy that is going to win this war? Many women are putting their lives on the line, doing countless jobs where one mistake will bring them certain death."

"And you, Madame, hiding behind your face covering. Am I to argue the morals of man with you or are we set to revise your plan to best suit the courage of the men in this room and that is to destroy the Germans?"

"Sir, I am not hiding my face to protect myself, but to protect you from insult from the Germans if questioned on my identity."

"I know of one other, one of great courage who demands respect for her contribution to her fellow Frenchmen, yet she revealed to me without fear as she knows of me and of my reputation."

The Swan hesitated.

"*Mes amis*, we are not here to argue points and throw daggers at each other," said Dante. "We are here for one single purpose."

"Yes, that is true, Dante," said Alfonso. "We know of the Swan's reputation as yours Fabre and neither is of question."

Fabre eased his stance and looked into the woman's eyes. He could see truth, and heart, and compassion as he had once looked into Marie-Madeleine's eyes. He had no recollection of seeing *these* eyes who peered through, hidden behind a scarf — only in a mad nightmare, a man at the break of frozen illusion, a character at an invisible table.

The Swan raised her hand and removed the scarf from her face. Alfonso let out a gasp as Fabre grabbed his arm to silence him. Fabre felt a warm rush flush over his body. *This is not possible! She who stands before me, I carried in my arms from the rubble of the Majestic Hôtel?*

"Are you satisfied, Fabre? May we now continue on," said the Swan rhetorically.

The Swan replaced her scarf and turned, and with Dante, they left Alfonso and Fabre at the chalkboard.

"Why did you not say something, Fabre?" asked Alfonso. "She is the woman who you risked your life for, and without gratitude."

"My friend, for now, let us not mention that ordeal. Say nothing to Daniel as he was the only other witness. She seems to want to keep her identity close to her heart. Let us not be the ones to expose her."

"Very well, Fabre. But she needs to know of what you sacrificed in saving her."

"We still don't know if she is an infiltrator for the Germans... as you saw and what you know...her fancy clothes and red lips and nylons. She dresses in disguises for a purpose."

"You have a very suspicious mind, Fabre. You found her nearest to death as one could be. And for Marie-Madeleine to trust her... should you not as well?"

"I hear what you say my friend, but my mind has its own way... sometimes without explanation to me."

The two men left the chalkboard and headed to the main hangar where the trucks and the rest of the Résistance fighters were gathered in a circle. The Swan stood in the middle. As Fabre and Alfonso approached, a *click-clack, click-clack* sound was heard. The fighters spun around from the circle and dropped to one knee with Sten guns pointing at the crack of moonlight sifting through the large hangar doors.

"What is that sound?" asked Fabre.

"My man," Alfonso said reassuringly, "...we got these clickers from the English. They sound like crickets when you press your fingers together against the metal device. It is a warning that someone is approaching."

Another single *click-clack* was heard and one of Alfonso's men slithered through the crack of the opened hangar door and waved his hand. Another man joined him and bent at his waist to his lack of breath. Alfonso waved the tired man in. The man straightened and trudged to the waiting fighters. He approached the Swan and whispered into her ear. She turned to Dante who brought the man to the trucks and gave him bread and some wine.

"*Mes amis*. We just received word of a caravan of trucks moving on back roads who were met by a division of Panzer tanks — probably the ones that held us up. To have such an escort, the cargo must be of great importance and I would surmise of what is missing here."

"That is only an assumption," said Fabre.

"And what would you assume, Monsieur Fabre?" said the Swan.

"We need more information of what is being carried and where it is going. I suggest we follow at a safe distance until we learn of the true mission."

"Your instinct is well-heeded, Monsieur Fabre. It is what we are to do. SOE will supply us further with information and more men and air support as needed. Until information of the rocket installation status is collaborated, we will observe and gather strength in numbers. Is the strategy to your liking, Monsieur Fabre?"

Alfonso nudged Fabre before Fabre had time to speak. Fabre just nodded. An urge to bow in grand gesture like a serf to his queen quickly vanished.

"Very well gentlemen, let us mount into the back of our trucks and put in practice of what our obligation to the effort has afforded us. We shall move the vehicles at five minute intervals!" the Swan said emphatically.

She turned to Fabre and looked him directly into his eyes and said, "Monsieur Fabre, may I ride up front with you?"

. . .

The moon had piqued as the caravan of freedom fighters picked up the trail of the Panzers that had held up the Swan and Dante's arrival at the airfield of Raketenflugplatz. The Swan had eased her back against the passenger door, resting with one foot on the steel dash and the other resting on the bench seat. Fabre and the Swan followed behind Alfonso and Daniel exactly five minutes apart as did the other trucks in the formation. The Swan had a hint of a smirk on her face as Fabre constantly eyed over to her.

"Monsieur Fabre, you should have more of a gaze on the road than you do on me."

"I am not gazing at you. I am checking the other mirror."

"As you say... but I can't help but feel a stare. Is there something you wish to discuss?"

"Nothing!" *Say nothing Fabre. Keep your eyes on the road,* he thought.

The Swan removed her foot from the steel dash and slid her leg under the other to get more comfortable and then she turned to Fabre. The moonlight cast a softness off of her face. Fabre noticed.

"Well then... when we first met in the hangar, you stared into my eyes as if you were reading my soul," the Swan said coyly — testing Fabre's resolve.

Fabre, don't answer her... just keep driving. See where she takes this.

"You deny it?" she asked.

Think Fabre... "I have peered into the eyes of a dream, an illusion, and a smile that warmth the imagination that no other words were needed." *Ah good Fabre. You are finally listening to me.*

"How romantic, Monsieur Fabre."

"Romantic in front of my name or behind my name or in the same sentence does not exist."

"Ha-ha, oh Fabre, you are a romantic."

How the hell did she translate that? "I am merely saying that words of love and such have not been in my heart, only hatred."

"But yet, you just spoke of love when your eyes met another. Is that not love?"

Okay mind... hello... where are you? Fabre was hard-pressed for an answer. He then said, "Not in the eyes of a man, no. Maybe out of concern, or duty, or the wish of another that bound one to duty."

"Ah, I see," said the Swan. She paused and then said inspiringly, "Have you ever flown in an airplane, Monsieur Fabre? It is exhilarating to fly up above the trees. It gives one a whole new perspective of life."

"No, I can say, I have not. And you have?"

"Yes! One of my first assignments was to ride in the open cockpit of a biplane crop-duster and as we flew over fields, we dropped whistle bombs. They were not filled with explosives but messages from de Gaulle for the Résistance. And then after completing each mission, I would have to parachute down and hopefully not get arrested or shot... or both."

"Why would you jump out of perfectly good plane?" asked Fabre.

"Because many of the flyers were caught as they landed and shot on the spot. One time, before a mission, I had secured a nun's habit as we were very close to a cloister. When I landed from the sky, I was too far from the forest so I tucked the parachute under me and had just finished hiding the last cord when a motorcycle with sidecar approached. The soldiers asked if I had seen a parachutist come down. I mentioned something like a sign from God and pointed to beyond a tree line that was in the opposite direction I intended on going. They politely nodded and roared off. I was very lucky on that one."

"You have a daredevil spirit."

"No!" she said, "...like you, a sense of duty."

Fabre smiled and looked over at the Swan who was twisting the ends of her scarf as she spoke, and then past her to the mirror.

"Your turn," said the Swan.

"For what?"

"To tell me about yourself. You must have many stories. What did you do before the war?"

"I was at the university studying finance. I had already opened a dry goods store and was making plans to travel the world seeking inspiring cloth to have available at my shop.

135

But since then and now as we are, I have another idea that would be much more profitable."

"And what would that be, Monsieur Fabre?"

"I was on a barge..." *Don't say saving your ass,* "...when an idea presented itself. As I watched the tedious work of the dock hands remove cargo and then re-stock the cargo on land in similar fashion, I came up with an idea of a cargo container that remained as one, full of whatever and then that could be lifted by crane to either be placed in a secured location or as a preset loaded onto rails for farther travel."

"And where would these containers go?"

"Anywhere... around the world."

"I see. You have a very astute mind. Do you also possess any other traits that require that kind of mechanical mind?"

"Before university I worked at a fabricating shop where I developed talent for welding and creating things from raw material."

"You are a very interesting man, Monsieur Fabre. And here we are, together, the farthest away from our dreams." The Swan sat up straight in her seat and pointed ahead. "Up here, take the 'Y' to the right. I have been this way once. To one side is forest and to the other is a large, open field. We must be careful as we approach. Look, Fabre! Alfonso's truck has stopped."

Fabre and the Swan slowed and pull up alongside of Alfonso's truck. No other explanation was needed as he and Daniel were in the middle of changing a front tire. A mist of warm air twisted and turned off of their backs in the pre-dawn hour.

"Stop! Please, Monsieur Fabre. My stomach is not at ease. Let us proceed on foot to beyond the 'Y' and scout the road ahead."

"You get these feelings often?" asked Fabre.

"I have had several. One as an 'out of body' experience where I could feel warmth and I was unafraid, and I felt the reassurance of being cradled in the arms of a passionate person... and then others, more of a sickening feeling."

"Which feeling is this one?"

"Sickening."

Fabre and the Swan had stopped the vehicle just ahead of Alfonso's truck and the two of them proceeded on foot to the 'Y' and before a tight curve. A whistle pierced the air and they dove for cover just short of a straight-a-way with the open field. A Panzer IV tank had stopped as well and its turret with its large barrel gun spun searching the skies. It stopped facing backwards, lowered its barrel and scanned the open field. A bomb had fallen but had not ignited. Two rounds were blasted off — the noise deafening. One zipped overhead of Fabre and the Swan and the other ripped out a tree in a massive explosion turning its trunk into match sticks and wavering fiber. Fabre covered the Swan's ears and held her tight, his full weight upon her.

The Panzer, satisfied that the bomb was a dud, swung its giant barrel around to face the front and its steel tracks dug into the ground, spitting out rectangular divots as it moved forward. The Swan raised her hands to Fabre's face and pulled him closer. She kissed him softly.

"What is that for? I merely forced you down to take cover."

"No, Fabre, it is a kiss of thank you."

"Again, woman, for what?"

"For saving my life."

"You mean after I almost killed you and then carried you in my arms to safety."

"Yes, exactly. You had no idea who I was or my mission. I had made peace, and that night was to be my last. But somehow, you managed to pull me to safety and you had no regard for your own in doing so. I have waited for this moment to say thank you — and I have waited patiently for you to swallow your pride and kiss me back."

Watch out Fabre. Say nothing. Kiss her, will you...

Fabre looked into her eyes and with his full weight upon her, he kissed her tenderly and passionately as he knew, and she knew, what was meant to be.

Fabre thought, *If this was not a war for survival created by a delusional nation of oppressors, I would scoop her up into my arms and carry her to the nearest cathedral and place her down at the concrete steps, then hand-and-hand walk up the steps to the wooden doors and inside we would stroll down the center aisle of hand-cut Italian marble to the foot of the alter and it would be there — I would declare my love forever.*

And the Swan smiled as she looked into Fabre's eyes and thought, *If I was not lying in these muddy tracks created by an imperialist army, coerced by a madman oligarch, I would jump into his arms and guide him to the nearest chapel and have him lower me to its steps so we may walk together side-by-side up the wooden steps and through the decorated arched doors, down the aisle that would be filled with a scatter of Jasmine petals, to the front of the alter where I would look into his eyes and pledge my endearing love — if only this were not wartime.*

"You look at me strangely. I am the same that you saved. Do I have mud on my face?" The Swan reached to her cheek without change to Fabre's face. She touched the wisps of blonde hair that poked out from under her Tam. "Is it my

139

hair? You don't like my natural color? You wish me brunette as you saw me?"

Careful Fabre. Another twist for you to unravel. Fabre looked longingly into her eyes and said, "Either! Your beauty is much deeper."

"Oh my!" chuckled the Swan. "You can say the right words when you want to. Now, promise me, Fabre... As you know, that one day, you will give me a girl."

"What...? Our first kiss, not even a night out with a meal and fine wine, and you want my child. Would not most men run at such a proposal?"

"I don't see you running," said Marta Savant.

Dante came up to the two on his hands and knees and whispered, "So, finally Fabre, you have met your match. Good luck to you, sir."

"You know the story?" asked Fabre as he eased off of Marta.

Dante stood tall and said, "Marie-Madeleine shared with us and only us, of your determination and dedication to bring the Swan safely back to us. No others know and thus must stay deep inside of us for everyone's safety."

"I hear you, man. Now help us up."

Dante shared his hand in friendship to Fabre and to the Swan.

"*S'il te plaît, Dante mon ami*, survey the situation with the Panzer for your safety, then retrieve the message from the whistle bomb," said the Swan.

"As you wish, *ma chère*."

Dante hunched down to the edge of the 'Y' and looked to where the Panzer had sat. All was clear. He crossed the muddy road, scarred with rectangular divots and went into the empty field to almost out of sight. Still behind the safety of the forest, Fabre turned to the Swan and said, "Is there anything I should know about with you two?"

"My Fabre, he is as close as a brother one could have. He is the proud father of five children and a beautiful plump wife, who I adore."

"You have known him a long time?"

"We have history. His kindness also saved me when I was most down and needed to regain my life. He shared his family with me, which raised my spirits and hope for the future. His wife, Jeanette, comforted me with a decision I had to make. She is remarkable."

"He watches you very closely," said Fabre.

"Yes, he was been my strength, but now, I have you," said the Swan putting her hand on Fabre's chest. "Come, walk with me; let us see if Alfonso has fixed the tire. When Dante returns we will have a better direction, I am sure."

"Like your Dante, Alfonso has protected my nephew. Look how he puts his back into the wheel wrench, and he spins the tire to be true. Alfonso is a dedicated man; an asset in many ways."

They looked back down the road with its bleeding vein of mud and ruts, quiet and surreal hidden by the forest protecting its brave men before they must turn at the 'Y' and the passage becomes treacherous and barren. Alfonso stood with Daniel admiring their worth.

"Alfonso... how is it going?" asked the Swan.

"The tire is of good shape and it spins true. We should be on our way momentarily, Madame."

"Thank you, my friend," said Fabre as he and the Swan swaggered back through the rutted road to their truck. The Swan opened the passenger door and retrieved a leather bound book.

"What is this?" asked Fabre.

"My journal... my journal of life and death... a recounting of things most dear and some not so," said the Swan.

"What do you write now?" asked Fabre.

"Of you... and us, and our future... that is... if you accept the challenge. And may I remind you, as we stand in these winter clothes, your vision of me is as if we holidayed at the beach in southern France."

"My vision of you, my dear, was of pure concern and not of pleasure, I assure you. However, as open as you speak, the vision was quite remarkable."

"Hahaha, oh Fabre, I am going to have a time with you, *n'est-ce pas?*"

"La Cygne! La Cygne! We must react quickly!" called Dante as he rushed to the Swan's side handing her the note. She read it to herself and then let out a gasp.

"What is it?" asked Fabre.

"*Mon Dieu*... Claus von Stauffenberg was gravely injured on the 7th *de Avril* and taken to Munich for surgery. I must go to learn of his health."

"Stauffenberg...? The Panzer commander? Why do you have concern for him?" asked Fabre.

"My darling, there is much for you to know. He has sympathies for the Résistance."

"How do you know this?"

"I was in Berlin before the incident at the Majestic. I was ushered into a private room away from a meeting that took place with von Stauffenberg, von Weißermann and another of even higher rank. They spoke in whispers of returning Germany to her glory and of not following the wishes of the *Führer* who was destroying the decencies of the Fatherland."

"But... why must you go?"

"We have met. He knows my involvement with von Weißermann to neutralize Hitler and his top officers, and the man who was instrumental in the development of the V-1 rocket program. Unfortunately, because of bad weather the scientist did not show at the Majestic."

"You mean, von Braun?"

"Yes. So you see my darling, I must go now. The letter also states for the rest of the team to continue on to the Baltic Sea to a place called *Peenemünde*. That area has become the center of activity for development of the rockets. Only observe, not to attack are their words, and send messages back to England for them to coordinate an air strike. Gage, will you do this for me and wait for me? I feel I have just found you and now I must say goodbye, but my heart is full."

"Are you sure the letter states that you must go to Stauffenberg or does it just inform you of his condition and we all must carry on?"

"I must go, my love. With all we have been through, there cannot be any doubt that von Stauffenberg will continue his pursuit of justice."

"Then, yes, I will do as you ask. And yes... I accept the challenge," said Fabre. He threw his burly arms around Marta and each hugged desperately.

"Go with her Dante and be her shield. We will find this Peenemünde and report of its events as you suggest. Be safe, my love, and write my name many times in your journal."

"Every page, Gage Fabre."

1 Mai 1943 - 11:30 Heures

Dante and the Swan had made their way to Berlin, obtained forged papers from the *underground* of her position of care under her real identity as entered on her medical school dossier. They continued their trek to Munich arriving safely. Infiltrating her way onto the staff of Ferdinand Sauerbruch, von Stauffenberg's surgeon, the Swan waited patiently for the opportune time to speak with Stauffenberg. His injures were severe, losing his left eye, right hand and two fingers from his left. But his humor was strong, jokingly saying that he never knew what to do with so many fingers when he still had them. The Swan was able to secure reassignment of her duties to the nightshift, away from most prying eyes. There was talk of von Stauffenberg being transferred to his home, a castle in the south of Germany. She had to make her move.

The corridors were quiet and the head nurse had just taken her break, the other nurse on duty was at the other end of the hall, away from Stauffenberg's room. The Swan took a long look down the hall and scampered quickly. When she arrived, she tapped lightly on the injured soldier's room. With clipboard in hand she entered.

"Herr von Stauffenberg," she whispered. "Do you remember me... Monsieur Claus? A friend of Herr von Weißermann, Marta Savant."

"Yes... yes of course, Mademoiselle Savant. How could I forget such a pretty face as yours? I had word, though, that you were dead. How is this possible?"

Marta slipped quietly over to Stauffenberg's bedside — their conversation private. She adjusted Stauffenberg's pillows.

"A miracle, I would say. But... you? When I heard, I came right away."

"That is very kind of you, Marta. I will heal, not all of me will go to my grave, but I will heal."

"The Aussies had no knowledge of your contribution and only a few who know of your brothers, know as I know."

"We should have stopped this madman in '42. I spoke of my displeasure in the mass shootings of the Jews to my friend *Joachim Kuhn*. I know we have backing but I must be in a different position, one of more power."

"I am so happy to hear this. You will be a hero to the people," said Marta.

"I will abide my time and heal quickly, I pray, and then we will see the opportunities play out. Tell them in England, not all is lost, only a little set back," smiled Stauffenberg.

Marta stepped closer and bent over the bedrail and gave Stauffenberg a gentle hug. "I must go now before anyone questions my disappearance. I will note in your chart of administrating you a sleeping sedative." She turned quickly and went to the door and slowly turned the handle. She stepped out.

Part way down the hall and to an adjoining corridor, the *clanking* of sharp *clicks* associated with the step of the Gestapo, rang through the hallways. The nurses' desk was on the other side of the corridor. Marta held tightly to her chart and scurried to her post. Two officers dressed in shiny, black-leather overcoats rounded the corridor and almost collided with Marta. She side-stepped them to avoid a collision. One tipped his hat in an apologetic manner while the other, stiff-faced continued into the direction of Stauffenberg's room. Then, the stiff-faced officer stopped, removed one of his black gloves and loudly snapped his fingers. Marta froze.

"Fräulein!" he shouted. "Have you just come from Lieutenant Colonel von Stauffenberg's room?"

Marta looked at the markings on the officer's shoulder. She replied, "Why yes, *Herr Obersharführer*."

"Is von Stauffenberg at rest?" he said coldly and rather disrespectfully.

"He is awake, but I gave him a sedative so he may sleep."

"Come hither!" he ordered, pointing his finger to the ground like a dog should obey.

Marta had one of her sick feelings but continued as requested.

"Your credentials, please," asked the kinder officer.

Marta handed her clearance and identification to the officer. He studied them carefully.

"You are from Belgium?"

"Yes."

"Your name is Claire?"

"Yes, that is correct, as it says," said Marta before the officer had a chance to finish.

"You have had no other?"

Mon Dieu, does he recognize me as Marta Savant...? "No... that is my Christian name."

"I meant... you are not married? One as pretty as you?" said the kinder officer somewhat flirtatiously.

"No," said Marta flatly.

"Come..." The rude officer grabbed Marta by her arm and ushered her through Stauffenberg's door. Entering, the two officers snapped their heels together in unison — crisp.

"Herr Lieutenant Colonel von Stauffenberg, we are sorry to intrude but do you know this woman?"

Stauffenberg looked at Marta. "Yes of course, she is one of my nurses. Why do you bother me with these questions?"

"Apologies, Herr Lieutenant Colonel von Stauffenberg, but do you know her name?"

Marta just about fainted... *He only knows me of my stage name... and I'm supposed to be dead...*

Stauffenberg looked into Marta's eyes. He knew if he said what he knew, she would be ushered out and probably shot. Instead, he turned the questioning around and shouted intensely, "You come in here in the middle of the night to ask me silly questions! Can you not see, man...? I am blind in one eye and suffer relapses and you want me to remember everyone's name that walks through these doors. Take it up with my chief surgeon... Now get out of my room!"

Oh, thank you, Herr Claus. You have probably saved my life, thought Marta.

"Sieg Heil!" they said in unison raising their arms skyward and clicking their heels – crisp.

. . .

Dante arrived a little early for the end of the Swan's shift and sat patiently outside the hospital as he did every morning before the sun came up. His eyes never abandoned and focused on the double glassed-etched doors. A black sedan car had arrived and two SS troopers had gotten out and entered. It was nothing new; always someone of no real importance had done as the ones now. But, after several minutes, as the doors swung open, Dante's heart plunged.

The Swan was in between the two SS troopers, small and fragile, dressed in white and worse — without weapons. The rear door of the sedan opened and the Swan was manhandled in. They sped off before Dante could swing his Sten gun up off the seat and let off a burst of fire, to at least slow them down. His mind raced. He turned his truck around and paced behind them as to not give notice. He felt his stomach aching, sweat beaded from his brow. His hands gripped the wheel tightly.

. . .

The days that followed in the month of May dripped with tears as Dante tried all of his resources to search out the whereabouts and fate of his beloved Swan. Dante had informed Fabre, through a courier, of the circumstance befallen them. Dante's words where true and that Fabre must

151

proceed with the plan and to be patient; not one of Fabre's finer qualities. In the note, Dante wrote of the SS interrogation strategies and hoped the Swan would remain faithful to the course that they had perceived in the event of such a fate.

. . .

The tears of May flooded the month of June without any intelligence on the Swan's state. Fabre, in his grief of losing Marta, headstrong and against the wishes of his fellow patriots, set himself up to be conscripted into the workforce at the Peenemünde Research Center. His reasoning, to give England firsthand knowledge of what was taking place and where. How could he deny the agony of losing Marta to not devote his life as well for the cause? Fabre's ideology, although debatable and met with resistance, was sanctioned. "His information would be invaluable," said England. Fabre's black and white striped coveralls shadowed his intentions.

. . .

It must have been the overbearing heat of July and the proven evidence time and time again, unaltered, tested but never wavering interrogations that the SS opened their doors to a drained and tired, and convincing nurse. The Résistance's paperwork had held up to the SS scrutiny. And the nurse's aliases – Marta Savant, cabaret singer, or more definitively, the Swan, were never in question.

Dante, on the night of July 21, watched as the Swan stumbled out of the doors at the SS headquarters in Munich. He screamed with joy, muffling his elation with his hands. Tears flushed his eyes as he saw his under-nourished comrade grab for the railing to sturdy herself as she took each step slowly and methodically. Dante pulled out of the alleyway and slowly approached the Swan and pulled to the street's curb.

Jumping out of his cab, he circled the front-end and came to her side and relinquished a huge hug upon her. He held her tight and said, *"Mon amour, je t'ai maintenant. Tu es en sécurité!"* She flashed a hint of a smile and knew she was safe now. Dante then supported the Swan with one arm and opened the door with the other. He helped her up, easing her into the cab and closed the door. Her body slumped into the seat and she rested her head on the door's glass window. Dante, after returning to his driver's seat, put his truck into gear and headed to safety leaving the injustice diminishing in the oval rear window.

Turning her head slowly to face Dante, her first words spoken were, "How is Fabre? Have you heard from him?"

"He has taken upon himself to infiltrate the research center with England's blessing. I believe he lost faith and thought he had lost you."

"Oh, no! He is a prisoner?"

Dante turned off the main thoroughfare to one of lesser traffic and drove down the street of flickering lamps in the pre-dawn light. He eyed his rearview mirror and slowed and said in a low voice, "He is working on the V-1's rocket line and sends messages through a discreet succession of individuals. He has devised a network to ensure if one caught, they would not dissect the whole network. Very clever of how he set it up. One man only knows of two others, the one that hands him the information and the one he hands the information to."

"Can we send word to him?"

"Unfortunately the network is one-way... for their protection."

"I see... but how will he know that I am safe?"

Dante looked over to the Swan. She had a more worrisome look on her face than before. "He has to know in his heart," he said.

The Swan turned her gaze out the side window; tears in her eyes. "Where are you taking me?"

"To a safe house so you may get strong and healthy."

"NO! Take me to where we said our goodbyes. Only there will he feel the connection. I will eat with the men and grow strength by their friendships."

"*Mon Dieu!* You are as obstinate as Fabre."

"I hope so, my friend. I hope he will feel my energy and he will conspire to leave this foolish decision of throwing himself to those dogs."

Dante looked over to Marta. Her passion was alight, her determination that grew inside of her even showed on her face with a little brightness. He shook his head knowing nothing else said would change her mind. Dante knew that Marta and Fabre's union was written in the stars.

2 Août 1943 - 12:20 Heures

Following country back roads and hit with delayed starts, unexpected stops and days and nights of camouflaged hindrance, Dante and the Swan managed to rejoin the Résistance and their friends, Alfonso and Fabre's nephew, Daniel, two weeks after the Swan was released from three months of intense interrogation by the SS. She was met with open arms and warm greetings.

The weakened state of the Swan was only suggested in closed groups and not mentioned out loud. She knew of the whispers but every day she exercised, ate as much as she could and exercised some more to regain her strength. Her naps seemed to always end in a perspiring startle of hot lights and sauerkraut breaths breathing into her face. But every day she would ask of Fabre's condition, without response. But this day, August 11 was different. She had received a message from England in one of their whistle bombs, of and according to information provided to them, that the RAF were plotting an air raid on Peenemünde. It was imperative that word be sent *in* to the patriots who were providing them with intelligence. Their lives and safety were at grave risk.

"How do we get word to Fabre?" asked the Swan after reading the message.

"It is a one way street," said Alfonso. "We never know when word will come out. We just wait for the courier and then notify an SOE agent who translates it to England by radio."

"There must be a way! The courier who comes here, can we contact him?"

"They are different every time. That is Fabre's beauty of his network," said Alfonso.

"I refuse to accept that as an answer!" declared Marta. "There must be a way?" She said as she walked in circles thinking, thinking like Fabre. *How did he set this up...?* She then stopped in her tracks. "Are the couriers timely?"

"They come at different times. Sometimes at thirteen hundred, sometimes at fourteen hundred hours, we never know."

"Yes you said that, but the days they come at thirteen hundred hours, is it an odd day or even day? And are the days four days apart or five days apart?"

Daniel stepped up as the other men were scratching their heads looking perplexed. "They come five days and six days apart. Last week on the 6th, the courier came at thirteen hundred."

"Very good, Daniel! So by this note from England they will send in a strike force on the 17th and by your calculations, Daniel, today at fourteen hundred hours a courier should arrive. That will give us five days to get word to Fabre."

The men looked at Daniel and wondered how he had deducted this regularity in the messages as none of it made sense and yet this young man had done just that.

"Please indulge me, Daniel. You see, my friends, my Fabre was sending another message all along. Each session, if you will, adds up to seven if you use standard time rather than military time, as we use to avoid confusion. Thirteen hundred hours becomes one and one plus six and five plus two... his lucky number of seven... he is alive and well. I know it!"

"Okay, say the boy is correct. What are we to send back that Fabre will believe?" said Dante.

"The courier recites numbers and characters but of no meaning to us. There is no paper with a transcript. If we send a written note, it could be compromised." said Alfonso, who was quickly interrupted by Dante.

"... and we still have no code to send back."

The Swan was thinking again, their words running through her head. *What would Fabre take as truth?* she thought.

Suddenly the Swan blurred out, "My scarf! Dante do you have my winter things in the truck?"

"Uh, yes. Everything is in the box."

"Good, please retrieve it for me. Fabre will remember our dual of words when we first... well, when we met again. I noticed a hand on Alfonso's arm as of recognition when I uncovered my face. He will believe me to be alive but also a warning of grave nature as no messages have been inbound."

"But he will not know what the message means and to act on it," said François who had been standing near.

"He will know enough, my friend. My Fabre will know enough," said Marta wistfully. "He will remember the cold, the near-death he felt, the dream of angels guiding him, and the peace of surviving. Yes, *mes amies*, he will know."

"Madame, a man approaches," said a comrade stepping to the small gathering.

"What time is it Alfonso?" asked the Swan.

Looking at his watch, Alfonso looked up amazed. "It is two."

Dante returned with Marta's scarf and handed it to her. The Polish courier recited his numbers and letters to Daniel who wrote them down. The Swan, not wanting to interfere with the transcribing waited patiently with excited eyes and a new energy. Daniel closed his book and the man was about to start off, but the Swan stopped him.

"Sir," she said, "can you get this scarf to the man inside?"

"Madame, my contact would have vanished by now."

"But you must have some knowledge of who you can give this to. It is life or death for thousands of detainees. You must try and help! We have only five days."

"Possibly the village near where I met the last courier. But how should I carry this and not look suspicious in the middle of a heatwave?"

"Do you have a lover?" asked the Swan.

"Yes, but..."

"Tie it around your waist and if stopped by the Germans and asked about the scarf, tell them your lover gave it to you so you might smell her perfume and then think about her," said Marta.

"That is almost true," said the young Polish man as he reached into his pocket and pulled out a small handkerchief. "She gave this to me with the same instructions."

The Swan smiled. "Yes, see? I want my man to do the same with my scarf."

"I will try, Madame. I must leave now and go quickly if I am at all going to meet up with my courier."

"Go in peace and please try with all you have," said Marta.

Alfonso turned to Daniel and said, "So when I ask you what you are doodling in your notebook and you say nothing, you are tracking Fabre's movement?"

"Well, sort of."

"What else?" asked the Swan.

"I have my version of what the code is saying."

"Your version, Daniel? Please enlighten us," said the Swan.

"Well, this last message said: 'come now... defense is low... 1:10... we will be ready.'"

"What!" said Alfonso. "You know this for how long?"

"Actually, today I finalized all the letters and signs," said Daniel.

"You are definitely Fabre's protégé, Daniel. I love you as a brother," said Marta, placing her arms about him.

Alfonso, the big man he is, put his arms about Daniel as well. "You have quite possibly saved my friend. I am in your debt now."

The others, one by one, came to Daniel and gave him hearty hugs. His respect amongst the fighters had doubled. He was no longer just Fabre's nephew; he was a man and a man of intellect.

"How will we know if Fabre receives your scarf?" asked Alfonso.

"We have to believe, my friend. We have to trust that Fabre's couriers also believe," said the Swan.

16 Août 1943 - 13:30 Heures

After Fabre put the last screw into the fuselage of the V-1 rocket at the Peenemünde Research Center, he was escorted away from the cranes that straddled four units — all to be delivered to a different partition that installed the war head. His sixteen hour shift had ended. His guard was sick and weak; almost a punishment to have to work in these conditions after being wounded. Hitler had no mercy for even his own men. Fabre could have bent this man in two but felt compassion. The German was not mean or demanding, just doing as he was told. There were nine other detainees in as sad shape as the guard; sickly, weak, malnourished and waiting to die. Their barracks stunk and laced with lice, no running water for showers and open latrines.

Archie, as Fabre called him, had his rifle slung over his shoulder, unable to support it on his bandaged, festering arm. He waited his turn to die along with whom he escorted to the wall-less barracks — primitive and isolated. A shout from behind had Fabre and Archie turning. A comrade of Archie's handed him a small package, unwrapped and whispered into his ear. As quickly as the comrade came, he turned and vanished out of sight. Archie trudged over to Fabre and handed him an object, tight and rolled. Fabre hid it in his stripped coveralls for his private observation. Too many eyes and too many loose lips could send a man to his death-bed just for an extra bowl of rice or a single fag.

The serving of their nightly meal, if it was at all night, was a mixture of rice and starchy corn infused with beans and separating milk added to sweeten the cattle corn, pooled with a brownish skim of whey.

The *clank* of unwashed forks against encrusted metal plates tumbled to the floor, which was routinely followed by mournful groans — all part of their nightly ritual. No washing off the day's sweat or yesterday's grime or the day before, infection lifting the fingernails to unbearable levels. Fabre, a strong man, a man of compassion bled inside for their pain. He found his spot, higher than most could reach or lift themselves to — broad boards removed from a parts pallet.

He removed his boots and laid them down to be used for a pillow. He turned to face the dusty gray concrete wall and reached into his coveralls for what Archie had given him. It was soft — he had noticed before. His fingers found an edge and in the dim light he started to unravel this mystery. As he

163

did, a scent flowed out as if a flower had been wrapped inside. He brought the material to his nose. A lingering taste, a welcoming smell, an over-whelming joy flushed his body. He cried out. *She IS alive!*

The others lay unconscious to anyone's plight — no matter the exaltation. Fabre was safe in his moment of relief. His mind swirled, each design shattered by another, pieced together, alternatives dismissed, scenarios played out with equal consequence. He held Marta's scarf tight. He felt for his etchings on the wall from his time of arrival and placed the next day's date at 17th *Août* if he were correct.

The hour of the day was uncertain as the ambient light, as dim as it was, had no bearing to daylight or twilight. He had seen no one with a watch and dare not ask a guard, even Archie. He then thought of his grand plan with his Polish couriers and how Marta must have reverse-engineered the use of Fabre's standard timing. In his excitement he counted the strokes on his wall going backwards from this day. For him to receive this scarf — and if his couriers remained with the plan — it was five days as he lay and roughly one hour for their meal and walking to their barracks. He assumed it was 1400 hours. He continued to map out his escape. Two hours plus eight hours before the next shift would place them back at work at 2200 hours.

An early morning raid under the guise of pre-dawn could possibly be between midnight and four; two to six hours into their work-day. He lay back with his arms and hands supporting his head feeling quite smug with himself. But his euphoria only lasted a moment. And then despair. *How will I be able to warn these men of what will definitely befall them? If I whisper to them now, that will leave fourteen hours that I could be betrayed. No, I must devise a plan. Maybe a diversion...*

17*th* Août 1943 - 22:25 Heures

The hours of the unknown weighed heavily upon Marta, and to see her Gage once more.

"I don't like this, Marta," said Dante in a whisper. "You are in grave danger if we are exposed so close to Peenemünde."

"You know I could not just wait to receive word if Fabre made it or not. Where would he go? We are all he has," she said pensively. "Besides, these corn fields under their noses will hide our movement."

"And as you say that, where is Daniel? I knew better than to let him come with us to this factory."

"Such as me, he has desire to lay eyes on his uncle. I could not deny him of that honor for as much as he has done to save Fabre."

"I know well the reasoning, just not the implication of such," said Dante.

"The moon is full and the night clear. It casts just enough light filtering through these large leaves — but not to expose one in the shadows before we are under cover of the forest."

Dante stood with knees bent and lifted his wrist past the five foot stalks, to the glimmer of the full moon, and marked his time at 22:30 hours. They waited quietly for any sound from the sky or one who might approach unwelcomed between the stalks.

. . .

Fabre purposely dropped his oil rag and slid between the hoisting cylinders to retrieve it. Out of sight, he spread open Marta's scarf. He had felt a thread relief and had not had an opportunity to visualize her message. He laid it upon the concrete floor and with the help of the overhead lights discovered the layout of the weapons factory. A silk 'X' marked his extraction point. He now had to translate what was sewn to what was reality.

Luckily, Fabre had been positioned at different stations of labor until his worthiness was suited to the heavy lifting and placing of the completed rocket onto the hoisting cylinders. He had a broad knowledge of the camp's layout — its intricacies not so much. He would improvise.

. . .

Dante was the first to turn from his belly to his back and look upward. Seconds later the Swan adjusted her body as Dante and she looked upward. Sirens began their *shrill* alarm. They waited for the search lights to scan the sky and the flak from the big guns, but none came. In the distance, they faintly heard the drone of engines.

"What is happening? Why have they not activated the searchlights?" The Swan asked anxiously.

"I don't know. Maybe they think it is a false alarm? Maybe they think who would be brave enough to attempt such a thing as to fly this far north? Maybe they think there is an attack on Berlin and if they illuminate the searchlights here, it will attract too much attention for Peenemünde?"

"But... it is truly happening, is it not?"

"The sound of the engines is getting denser. I would say... YES!"

"Thank God! I shall get my Fabre back!" exclaimed the Swan.

The RAF's Lancaster bombers dressed with four Rolls-Royce 'Merlin' engines started to shatter the night's air. At 23:30 Berlin time, the first tracer bombs dropped at Peenemünde. The roar of the Merlin engines was steadily increasing. Then the heavy-weight bombs started to fall by the dozens and explode seconds apart. More and more bombs, too many to count and a fortress of planes filled the

167

skies. Their underbellies camouflaged but their yellow tail markings, illuminated by the full moon, shone like brilliant stars to Dante and the Swan.

Their jubilance was short-lived as several bombs missed their mark south of their intended target. Rows of corn fields that dotted the landscape were destroyed sending mounds of dirt spraying over Dante and the Swan's bodies. Fear rang louder than the bombs themselves — their hands cupped their ears. Engines *growled* and bombs *whistled* and then *exploded* at one hundred and fifty decibels mere yards from where they lay. An armada of over five hundred planes flew over them at ten thousand feet. The ground shook and trees swayed back and forth in a wave from their intensity. The sounds of the explosions moved slightly north and soon, the planes dissipated into thin air as quickly as they had arrived.

The Swan's heart was heavy. She knew what destruction had just occurred. Lives obliterated. Families lost. Sons and daughters became orphaned and homeless. The tragedies of war — and for what gain? The Swan lifted her head and looked forward to where a twenty-foot wall used to stand. Bricks and mortar, concrete and re-bar lay side by side without distinction. Barbed-wire, once proudly laced like fine French lingerie, crushed beneath. What could one hope to find in this carnage?

Dante helped the Swan to her feet. Clumps of roots embedded with dirt fell to the ground. They each stood

John F Russo

supporting each other, hope abandoned, tears streaking their muddy faces in long ribbons — droplets depositing explosive clear pearls upon their boots. Dante looked around in astonishment. The corn field despoiled and cratered with twelve-foot deep tombs — stalks smoldering in black ash.

In the silent aftermath, Daniel, who stood some twenty paces in front of Dante and the Swan, hollered out, "Look!" He pointed. A bloodied hand reached for the top of the concrete pile and pushed aside a small cluster of blocks causing it to *click-clack* as it rolled down to the beaten foundation. A head popped above that. There was no mistake. Fabre crawled with all his might and tossed himself over the destruction and rolled down its massive mountain to be cradled by the spared few remaining rows of standing stalks.

Daniel set-off afoot towards his uncle, arms spread like an Orangutan — beating at the stalks, and legs barreling through until he reached Fabre's side. Only momentarily inspecting Fabre's injuries, he lifted Fabre up and supported him as they trudged back toward Dante and the Swan. Moments later another hand, bloodied as Fabre's, appeared from behind. The figure lifted himself from the rubble. His uniform torn, his spectacles cracked in a sunburst, the soldier yelled at Fabre to stop or he would shoot. His black boots found a foothold and he raised his rifle.

"*Stoppen sie den gefangenen! Ich werde schießen!*" he yelled again.

Fabre looked straight ahead. The golden tassels swayed in the moonlight as they, Fabre and his nephew Daniel, plowed through. Dante and Marta caught up and helped to support Fabre just as a shot rang out. Dante quickly raised his Sten gun, turned toward the concrete mound and rattled off a barrage of fire power with a sweeping motion. Shattered bullets sparked against the gray matter sending divots of concrete whipping — others found their intended target. The soldier swaggered to his knees, his eyes blurred and he fell backwards out of sight. Fabre felt Daniel's hand as strong as it was, become weak and nimble. Daniel collapsed without a word.

Fabre turned. He looked down and into the dying eyes of his nephew. Fabre bent to him and cradled him, rocking him back and forth and Fabre's tears washed his face and his anguish distorted his face — Fabre's Daniel, not a cry as he looked up at his uncle, his hand holding tight to Fabre's — his eyes big and bright as he took his last breath. Marta sunk to her knees. Her arms held Fabre cradling him, and Fabre cradled Daniel. Fabre's only family, his nephew, his love, the only one left had saved him from a Nazi's bullet. A promise made in the past held no integrity now.

The midnight moon drifted. The golden tassels lost their glow as Fabre shouldered his Daniel and they all headed for the protection of the forest.

20 Août 1943 - 12:00 Heures

Fabre had laid his nephew, Daniel, in a marked grave with a fabricated white cross at the intersection where Alfonso had blown a tire and the pasture met the forest. It was when they were all together — where Marta confessed her love for Fabre and Fabre in turn. It was where they looked into each other's eyes before the whistle bomb dropped and where the Panzer tank unloaded two shells. It was there at that spot before the note from England confirmed the injuries of von Stauffenberg and Marta had to re-confirm his devotion to the demise of Hitler. This is what Fabre wanted to remember.

He had remarked while standing over the grave, "My heart is black — my veins are flushed with fuel ready to ignite. But here, I am calm, saluting a boy who became a man, a nephew who grew wise before my eyes. He has granted me my life, and I shall be eternally grateful for this gift."

Heads hung — eyes misty — each in turn tossed the black dirt onto the white rocks. Words were muttered to the ability of each man and each man took a swig of wine and swished it about and in a circle around the grave, each man spat it out to protect the fallen. The ceremony was neither religious nor rehearsed.

It was as it was, draining and yet uplifting, anxious yet calming, words spoke of truth, not imagined with flowery antidotes as Daniel the boy — as Daniel the man — and no more.

7 Mai 1945 – The End of WWII

The last two years of the war, Marta never left Fabre's side. They endured pain, and more loss, friends died in front of them and yet – they survived.

Claus von Stauffenberg was implicated in the *Valkyrie* plot of July 20th. 1944 to assassinate Hitler and he was shot. His brothers and high ranking generals were repeatedly strangled, resuscitated and then finally hung.

Atrocities were unearthed and judged, and yet over 1600 SS scientists who destroyed countless lives were scooped up and made into American heroes. Hitler's space program now deemed NASA.

Dante returned to his family and Marta returned to Paris with Fabre. They capitalized on several of Fabre's designs and ideas. Their ages were still young, but their minds had lived a hundred years. They consoled each other when their dreams became more than one could bear. Nights awoken, rocking in each other's arms until the tears eased.

Août 1976

It has taken many, many years to be able to transcribe what we have seen — what we have lived through. This Journal has been written with truth of observation, with the help of Fabre and his memory, and friends who walked beside us.

And the purpose is two-fold:

First, to ease the demons from our collective minds and placed on paper the events that shaped us.

And secondly, to share our life with you both, so that you will understand and know that your journey, although it might not be smooth or going to your order, but trust in your intuition and realize that centurions have been placed at every possible point — a nudge here, a nudge there, a friendly smile, a helping hand when most needed. A letter to you separate from these pages will be placed at your disposal and discretion to read.

Take serious the spies of your era and sympathizers of Odessa — their off-spring are saboteurs who have been cloned in hatred and raised amongst us. They are disguised as politicians and patriots who are bent on destroying our fabric of life. They are leaders of corporations that create drugs to kill us openly, who diminish our food with poison. They have an arsenal of lies to tarnish the reputation of the ones you love most.

Your family has attempted to protect you from outside interference from these criminals. Please, be aware they are real and do exist. You will know when the time is right and hopefully, your training has taught you well.

Your code names have been well-established, preserved, and feared.

We love you, my darlings...

AUTHOR'S NOTES

The idea for delving back into Angela's ancestry seemed like a natural direction as her stories become more complex. I know I had a desire to try and understand her motives. On the onset, Le Journal was to be a mere few pages, a couple of discoveries that would be mentioned in the next book, Whiteburn. But, I concluded that the story needed to be heard in a grander spectrum.

As a found journal in the cellar on the property of Claire's Sanctuary, one wonders what secrets it must contain to be hidden in such an anonymous location. Did Claire (Marta Savant) unravel the secrets that Sister Bernadette told her about? Is what's inside not meant to be shared with outsiders?

The unique Cryptex lock that latches the leather bound journal holds another hint of ancient mystery. How does this all play out? And most importantly, does Angela believe any of it? What is the reference to "you both"?

Scene: when Fabre enters Matteo's barge and they sit down to drink wine. The scar on Fabre's left arm was an accident I had working on a hot rod. The grinder did spin around and I had to step on the electrical cord to be able to grab it.

Claire Marie Sonnet was my Belgium-born grandmother's name. She met my grandfather, an English soldier during WWI. She was vibrant and loved to sing and dance.

The original Majestic Hotel was occupied by the Nazis in Paris. It is very eloquent not at all the way I describe *my* Majestic hotel.

The names of the streets are what they were called pre-WWII. After liberation, the names were changed to honor the Generals of the leading allied forces.

Marie-Madeleine Fourcade was barely thirty years old when she took over running the largest Résistance spy ring in France. She had been arrested twice by the Gestapo and escaped both times. She died on July 20, 1989.